Story of the Year 2

the ten winning stories

THE INDEPENDENT

the ten winning stories

Ann Burnett, Maggie Butt,
Norma Clarke, Sara Conkey,
Graham Laurence, Charles Lowndes,
Finbar O'Connor, Robert H Richard,
Alan Stone, Sean Taylor.

SCHOLASTIC

Scholastic Children's Books,
Scholastic Publications Ltd,
7-9 Pratt Street, London NW1 0AE, UK

Scholastic Inc.,
555 Broadway, New York, NY 10012-3999, USA

Scholastic Canada Ltd,
123 Newkirk Road, Richmond Hill,
Ontario, Canada L4C 3G5

Ashton Scholastic Pty Ltd,
P O Box 579, Gosford, New South Wales,
Australia

Ashton Scholastic Ltd,
Private Bag 92801, Penrose, Auckland,
New Zealand

First published by Scholastic Publications Ltd, 1994

Text copyright © the authors, 1994
Illustrations copyright © the illustrators, 1994

ISBN 0 590 54172 2

Typeset by A J Latham Ltd, Dunstable
Printed in England by Clays Ltd, St Ives plc

10 9 8 7 6 5 4 3 2 1

Contents

Introduction

Welcome to *Story of the Year 2*! In this anthology you will find the ten winners of the 1994 *Independent*/Scholastic Story of the Year Competition. Last year's competition was the most successful the *Independent* has ever run, and this year's response was just as phenomenal – nearly 2,500 writers sent us their stories for six to nine-year-olds. Once again, the editorial team at Scholastic were swamped with manuscripts to be carefully read, judged and reported on. And eventually, the 2,500 were narrowed down to twenty. Then it was up to the five judges to select the final ten: Terry Jones, writer, film director and former member of Monty Python; Anne Fine, the children's writer, whose books include *Madame Doubtfire*; David Fickling, editorial director of Scholastic Children's Books; Julia Eccleshare, children's literature correspondent of the *Bookseller*; Enid Stephenson, vice-chair of the Federation of Children's Book Groups; and Blake Morrison, author and journalist. Selecting the final ten was no easy matter – although *Dear Norman* was always the unanimous favourite. However, after much wrangling, arguing and soul-searching, the two runners-up and the seven finalists were chosen.

The aim of this yearly competition is to give children who are reading alone for the first time a real thrill, to excite them, and make them think: I'm glad I read that – I want to read more. We wanted to draw attention to the enormous formative importance of writing for these early readers – the six to nine-year-olds. And more than that – to celebrate the idea of the storyteller and to provide an encouraging platform for writers for this vital age who might not previously have had the chance to be heard.

We at Scholastic think that the chosen winners of the Story of the Year Competition represent the very best traditions of storytelling. We looked for fresh,

INTRODUCTION

original, sparky stories, stories which draw in the reader – and we found in the ten finalists these qualities in abundance. We would like to congratulate the overall winner, Robert H Richard, for the highly original *Dear Norman*; the two runners-up, Sean Taylor and Sara Conkey; and *all* the writers in this book for ten excellent, varied stories.

Once again, happy reading!

Scholastic Children's Books

Winner

Dear Norman

ROBERT H RICHARD

Illustrated by
NICK SHARRATT

For Jason, Iris, Erin, Max, Alex, Whitney,
Luke, Avery and Lily

Dear Norman,

Thank you so much for your letter which arrived just before lunch.

It came as quite a surprise when you left with all of your possessions this morning. We did not understand why you left through the back door. Now we know that it was because you have gone to live in your tree house in the back garden.

I am sure that your decision to leave our family is a serious one. Therefore I would like to wish you all the best for the exciting new life you are starting on your own. Please do keep in touch from up there.

Love,
Dad

Dear Norman,

You are very sweet to take the time to write. Thank you for explaining a few of our mistakes in such detail. Your father and I will find your advice very useful as your sister grows up.

I hope that life in your tree house is calming down since you moved in earlier today. I could see from the dining room how difficult it was to carry all your things up that long, steep ladder by yourself. How did you manage to get that big TV set up there? It certainly was clever. Now how will you manage to get electricity for it? I'll bet you have another clever idea!

Did you see those sweet, busy bees swarming around below your tree house porch this afternoon? I suppose they could have been hornets or wasps building a nest, but they looked more like jolly little bumblebees to me.

No doubt you took plenty of food with you up into your tree house. I'm afraid I didn't plan the day as well as you, so I have this extra cheese sandwich and a chocolate bar left over. I am sending them up your message rope with this letter in the hope that you can use them in some way.

If you think of any other mistakes your father and I made don't hesitate to get in touch.

Meanwhile, lots of love from
Mum

Dear Norman,

Mum and Dad say I can have your room. Ha ha.

Beth

Dear Sir/Madam,

The book you recently ordered: *How To Negotiate*, has now arrived. We will hold the book for you in our shop for 7 days.

Thank you for your order.
The Parkville Book Shop

Dear Norman,

I understand from your parents that I should not expect to see you in school for some time due to changes in your personal life. Please take as much time as you feel you need.

Perhaps school no longer seems important now that you live in a tree house behind your family's home. That makes sense. Geography, Music, History: which of the lessons you missed this morning would be useful in a tree house? None, probably.

What you need are different skills, skills useful for life in the wild: How to keep a small, safe fire burning for light and warmth. How to tell good berries, nuts and mushrooms from deadly ones. Which animals you will compete with for territory. Unfortunately, we don't study any of these at Parkville School. You will have to do most of your learning on your own now, Norman.

If you decide to continue any of your studies with us please send me a note. I cannot send you all of the fun and friendship from our class here at Parkville School, but I can certainly send you the homework!

All best wishes from me and from all your classmates in Room 214.

Mrs Bouquet

Norm,

You don't know me very well but I've seen you around. My message is: go for it. Don't let them push you around. Stay up in that tree house until you get what you want.

Your fan,
Daniel Barleycorn

Dear Norman,

Thank you for sending me your photograph. You look like a typical Western boy! Here is my photograph. Maybe I look like a typical Japanese girl?

I am glad we are pen pals. Now I can practise my English. Do you want to practise your Japanese? Ha ha.

I am also glad that writing letters is your favourite hobby. What luck for me!

Your Pen Pal,
Mariko

Dear Norman,

I hope you don't mind me putting this message on your rope. I am the guy who has come to fix your family's refrigerator (that's my blue and white van in the drive). Although we have never met I am writing you this note because I moved into my own tree house once when I was a kid. I can't remember the reason.

Anyway, I want you to know that you have my support.

Darryl, Refrigerator Engineer, 38 years old

Hey Kid,

Pull yourself together.
You're making a fool of yourself.
Surrender now.
They'll take you back.
Trust me.

Signed,
Anonymous

Dear Norman,

I hope you are well and not spending too much time worrying about your lonely old grandmother. I'm fine most of the time. I do have bad days when none of my grandchildren have visited or telephoned, but I try to remain cheerful.

Your mother says you have been acting strange lately. Stop it; that's not polite.

Next time you speak to my son (your father), please tell him from me (his mother, your grand-mother) that it's high time he wrote a letter to his mother (me).

I'm so glad you liked the sweater I sent for your birthday. I had to spend half the day crossing town to get it, and of course it was not cheap. Still, it was worth it if you appreciate it so much.

I can't wait to see all of you next weekend. You are what keeps me happy!

> *Love,*
> *Grandma*

Hey Norm,

What's this about you living in your tree house now? Totally cool! Does this mean you can eat whatever you want? Stop washing? Stop brushing your teeth? Are you going to wear the same clothes every day for a year? Just think: you can spend the whole night playing with your Gameboy! You can stay on strike for months! This is so cool. I wish I had thought of it.

> *Alfred*
> *P.S. Can I have your bike?*

Dear Occupant,

I am writing to you today with a very special offer. We at Family Publications would like to send you the next twelve months of *Good Boy* magazine for only £4.99. What a deal! That's only 42p per issue!

For only 42p you get *Good Boy* magazine every month. Each issue is packed with ideas to help you become the perfect son and brother:

- *How to help your sister do the dishes.*
- *Cleaning up your room before Mum asks.*
- *Enjoying garden chores.*

Plus there are our regular features: "The Polite Crossword", "Thank You Letter of the Month", and "Table Manners".

Do your entire family a big favour: order today. Don't miss another month's issue of *Good Boy* magazine!

But wait! That's not all! If you order now we will also send you – absolutely free of charge – a *Good Boy* baseball cap. Wear it and all your friends will know what a Good Boy you are!

Why not be a Good Boy today?

Order now.

Yours sincerely,
The Marketing Department
Good Boy Magazines
Family Publications

Dear Norman,

Your pest of a sister told me on the bus today that you have moved into your tree house and aren't coming to school any more. How are we going to sit together on the bus and meet at lunch if you won't come to school?

Daniel Barleycorn wants to go out with me. I said no because I'm going out with you. Now I'm not so sure. If you and I can't talk on the bus and meet at lunch, there is nothing left of our relationship. Will you be installing a telephone in your tree house? A fax? I doubt it.

I think our relationship has reached a turning point. This is curtains.

I am truly sorry.
I will always love you.
Eileen x x x

Dear Norman,

> You are invited to a Birthday Party
> for Alison Child –
> The most beautiful girl in our school.
> Refreshments & Possible Kisses.
> Saturday, 11 May, 5 pm.
> RSVP

Dear Norman,

Thank you for your letter explaining why you do not want any pocket money this week. It made your mother and me wonder how much we would save if you continue this practice for the remainder of your childhood.

10 years x 52 weeks per year x £2 per week pocket money = £1,040 total savings.

(You might want to check our maths.)

Isn't it amazing the way it adds up?

Love,
Dad

Dear Norman,

Congratulations! Your essay "Peace Now" has won First Prize in *The Parkville Gazette*'s Solving the World's Problems Contest! The judges were especially impressed by the section "Peace Begins in Your Own Back Garden".

As you know, the First Prize in the Solving the World's Problems Contest is a trip to Washington D.C. where you will visit the White House and actually discuss your essay with the President of the United States. You will be able to take one member of your family with you on this once-in-a-lifetime trip.

Please ask a parent or guardian to contact me as soon as possible to make arrangements for the trip.

And congratulations once again on your wise essay!

Best wishes,
The Editor
The Parkville Gazette

Norman,

Dad said I should write. I miss you. I think you should move back into our house. I don't think you should be on strike any more. It's boring.

I haven't decided yet about letting you have your room back. We can negotiate.

> *Yours sincerely,*
> *Your sister,*
> *Beth*

Dear Norman,

Thank you for your letter. I understand your feelings. It will be okay just to move back into the house. Don't forget to wipe your feet.

> *Love,*
> *Mum*

ROBERT H RICHARD

Robert Richard was born in the USA into a large family. Until eight years ago he moved around America and Europe, growing up, studying and working. Now he lives and works in Kent, where he is a director of a company which specializes in English language training. He is currently involved in developing a CD-ROM product for children, but Dear Norman *is his first piece of children's published work. It was originally written as one of the stories he regularly sends to America to entertain his many nieces and nephews.*

He says: "Everyone appreciates children's love of magic in stories – their readiness to accept purple cows, talking houses or time travel without a flicker of disbelief. I am more interested in their response to the magic tricks of narrative itself: how, for example, this story can be about Norman without a single appearance from Norman. Or how a series of letters alone can tell a story without any bossy, grown-up narrator. Kids' eyes just stay open wide through it all, drinking it in. They accept and absorb a story's 'rules' without question. They say 'of course' (if they say anything at all) and simply want to hear what happens next. Theirs is an impatience for which I am grateful."

Runner-up

The Tale of the Bad Ship Torment

SARA CONKEY

Illustrated by
PETER BAILEY

For Gill

It was dawn on board the bad ship *Torment*. Captain Razelbreath raised a telescope to his one good eye. The sea was blue and empty: the *Torment* was alone on the wicked high seas. Captain Razelbreath lowered the telescope and laughed his especially terrible laugh. It was a cross between a vulture's cry and a creaky wardrobe door and if you have never heard that, it is pretty terrible. For Captain Razelbreath had made a huge fortune by terrorizing his way around the oceans of the world. If other ships spied the bad ship *Torment* in the distance, they quickly scooted off in the opposite direction. Razelbreath ruled supreme and that was the way he liked it.

Quickly, Razelbreath made his creaky way into the bowels of the ship. Down and down he went, past the snores of the still-sleeping sailors. Finally, he stopped at the deepest, darkest door. He looked to the right and to the left, then pulled out a long thin key on a chain from underneath his long thin cloak.

In a flash he was inside.

The room was dim for it was lit only by a tiny porthole and a candle. It was in this room that the captain kept his one and only love: the Princess Marie-Rose. He had stolen her on a stormy night from the ship of a duke, and of all his treasures, it was she who he prized the most. But despite all his best attempts, the princess had ignored him from the day she had been captured. She had eaten nothing, although Razelbreath arranged for the most tempting food to be brought to her. She had only said, "I cannot eat and I cannot love."

Marie-Rose was sitting, as she always sat, in a chair of cream, dressed in a dress of dark green silk. Her dark eyes were fixed on the one patch of blue glowing in the only porthole.

It infuriated Razelbreath beyond belief that she could ignore him so completely. For if there's one thing a cruel and heartless sea-captain cannot stand, it's to be ignored. Razelbreath liked a lot of attention. He threw a chair at the wall, he threw a cushion at the ceiling and stamped his foot very,

very hard. But Marie-Rose sat perfectly still in her green silk dress and simply said, "I cannot eat and I cannot love."

Razelbreath growled, "Have it your way!" And in a flash he had locked the door again.

Razelbreath always kept the key to the princess's room on a chain around his neck, for the captain had a secret and deadly fear.

When he was seven and practising his wickedness by tormenting toads, he met an old woman whose pet toad he had just mangled in a rather disgusting way. The old woman was so furious she put a curse on Razelbreath: "Wicked you want to be and wicked you shall be, Morton Razelbreath, but if the one you love loves another, before you persuade her to marry you, the spell of your fear will be broken and you will become as small and unimportant as that toad you so cruelly tormented."

Razelbreath shuddered when he remembered the witch's words – as he did every morning – and he was clutched by the iron hand of fear.

"If she loves another . . ." he whispered. But no, that was impossible, for she saw no one and the only key was around his own scrawny neck.

She will stay there until she loves me – or starves!

Razelbreath thought, as he reached the top of the stairs and smiled horribly.

"Work harder or you'll be a shark's breakfast!" he bawled and kicked a sailor who was scrubbing the deck.

The crew of the bad ship *Torment* hated and feared Captain Razelbreath. Quite often he would say, "Work harder or you'll be a shark's breakfast!" and then have a poor sailor thrown overboard just to prove he meant it. The sharks followed the *Torment* all over the wicked high seas, because they knew it was a good meal ticket. And so the crew worked harder and harder, and shivered when Razelbreath passed creakily by.

But there was one crew member who was not afraid of Captain Razelbreath. His name was Simon and he was the assistant cook.

He was the smallest and youngest of the crew members. Simon completely ignored Razelbreath's rages: he merely sighed and carried on cooking. For Simon was secretly a master chef: he was forced to cook the stews and soups of sailors' fare, but he dreamed of one day making cherry flans and strawberry fools and scrumptious salads.

At that moment, the captain burst into the

kitchen. Simon had just made a plateful of steaming ginger and cinnamon biscuits and proceeded to get them out of the oven. Razelbreath watched the boy with his one good eye.

"Stand still boy, or you'll be a shark's breakfast!"

"Yes, Captain," replied Simon. "I just thought you might like to try a biscuit."

He held one out to the captain.

The captain snatched the biscuit from the boy's hand and gobbled it in one terrible gulp. Then a curious expression spread over the captain's face: somewhere between a grimace and a glare. He grabbed the plateful of biscuits and tipped them into his mouth and down his throat in one go. In two seconds they were all gone, with only a few crumbs left on the plate to show they had ever been.

Razelbreath wiped his mouth with his one good arm and eyed the boy carefully. He had thought of a cunning and terrible plan.

"Boy, make three irresistible meals by sundown or you'll be a shark's supper." And with that he made his creaky way out of the kitchen. Simon could hardly believe his luck! A free hand to cook what he liked! So while Simon weighed and rolled and sieved and chopped, the captain paced and grunted and sniggered and growled, and somewhere far, far below in the bowels of the ship, the Princess Marie-Rose stared at the only porthole and sighed a large sigh.

The sun had set. Razelbreath creaked into the kitchen. He half hoped the boy hadn't succeeded in making the three irresistible meals, for then he could throw him to the sharks. But Simon was standing there with three platters covered in linen cloths.

The captain pulled back the first cloth. A riot of colour invaded his one good eye – it was a ship made of every kind of fruit you could possibly imagine – golden peaches were the planks, strings of sliced apples were the ropes, half melons were the sails, and a perfect strawberry the anchor. Razelbreath's eyes were as big as plums.

Quickly, he pulled away the next cloth to reveal a small and perfect turkey, bathed in honey, succulent and juicy beyond imagining. Razelbreath sniffed in ecstasy.

The third platter revealed a pie – and what a pie! It looked as if it was made of clouds. It was swirly and curly like a soft white sea. It smelt of lemons and heaven. A silver spoon lay beside it, invitingly. Razelbreath sighed.

But instead of tucking in without further ado, to Simon's surprise the captain re-covered the food, whisked away the platters and disappeared from the kitchen. He returned an hour later with the empty platters, growling the words, "Boy, make three irresistible meals by tomorrow sundown, or you'll be a shark's supper."

And so it went on, day after day: Simon cooked and baked and stirred – Razelbreath entered and swooned with delight, whisked away the food and returned with the same instructions. But Simon was exceedingly curious. Who was eating his delicious food?

So the next night when Razelbreath had taken away the three platters, Simon followed him. It was dark on the ship, so the captain did not notice Simon's stealthy footsteps and slim shadow. He slipped through the side door just behind the captain. Down and down they went – Simon had never been so deep into the ship before. At last, around the deepest and darkest bend, the captain stopped. He drew out a long silver key which glittered in the early moonlight. Then he was gone. Simon leaned against the wooden wall, his breath coming hard. He knew that if he was caught, he

would be fed to the sharks piece by piece for breakfast, dinner and supper. But still he had to know.

Silently, he crept up to the door and lowered
his eye to the keyhole. And there he saw a sight
that made his elbows quiver and his knees melt: the
most beautiful girl he had ever seen was delicately
spooning his turtle-shell soup into her delicate pink
rosebud mouth.

Her dark eyes were sparkling with happiness as
she tasted the hundred subtle flavours. Her dark
thick hair seemed to get thicker and darker, and her
white cheeks, starved of sunlight for so long, glowed
fresh pink. Razelbreath was watching her, greedily.

But when she had eaten the last morsel of walnut
cake, the princess pushed away the platter, turned
and stared at the handful of stars she could see
through her only porthole and said, "I cannot love."
Razelbreath smiled his most horrible smile. He had
succeeded in making the princess eat – it
was just a matter of time before he made her love!
He fell to his knees and begged her to marry him.
But the princess only said, "I cannot love," and
ignored him as completely as if he were invisible.

Simon sped back to the kitchens – and not a
moment too soon. Razelbreath creaked through the

door, flung the platters on the floor and growled, "Three irresistible meals by sundown, or you'll be a shark's supper."

But Simon was inspired! Now he had seen the princess he pushed himself to greater and greater heights. Everything he made, he made with the image of Marie-Rose before his eyes. Every pot of cream he whipped, he whipped with love. He made swans of icing sugar, ginger-bread flowers, houses made of treacle cake and orange blancmange cats. And whatever he made, the Princess Marie-Rose ate.

He made hearts of strawberries, baskets of apricots, chocolate faces and apple crumble. And whatever he made, the Princess Marie-Rose tucked into.

He made boats of ice-cream, elephants of marzipan, cherry lemonade and blueberry pie. And everything he made, the Princess Marie-Rose polished off.

Now love is a strange thing. People can say "I love you" until they are blue in the face and sometimes they mean it and sometimes they don't. But when someone cooks with love, you can taste it straight away.

And so it was with Marie-Rose. When she sipped

Simon's cherry lemonade, she knew he loved her. When she tasted his orange blancmange, she knew he adored her, and when she tucked into his blueberry pie, she knew he worshipped her. Each main course was a love-letter and each pudding a love song. And she began to melt.

The day this happened was at dawn one summer morning. Razelbreath was making his creaky way down to check that his princess was still safely under lock and key when he began to feel a little shaky. He took another step and began to feel a little quaky. He sat down on a step and felt sick.

Razelbreath was no fool. He knew something had happened. The princess's heart was melting.

Razelbreath began to think hard – how could anyone have got to Marie-Rose? He kept her locked in the deepest, darkest part of the ship, and he kept the only key around his own scrawny neck. He took every morsel of delicious food to her with his own hands, and watched her eat it all alone.

Suddenly Razelbreath saw black. He got up, he raged, he ranted.

He cried out, "I have been far too nice for far too long!"

Then he stormed down the stairs to the deepest

darkest door and opened it with a cry. He grabbed Marie-Rose roughly and forced her out of the door and up the wooden steps. On the deck in the bright sunshine, Marie-Rose tottered and almost fell. Razelbreath grasped her roughly to his thin side. He called all the crew to him. They stood quaking before him.

"Today," he announced, "the Princess Marie-Rose and I are going to be married."

The crew gasped.

"We will have a huge wedding breakfast and we'll eat and drink all day."

The crew cheered.

"But first," Razelbreath smiled his most vicious smile, "our fishy friends must share our wedding celebrations."

With that he grabbed Simon by the collar with his one good arm and fixed him with his one good eye.

"It is a pity, my boy, that it will not be your apple crumble we shall be scoffing on my wedding day —" then he whispered in the boy's ear, "The princess has grown to love your pies and pastries — soon she will love you. But sadly, before that happens, we will be married and you will be a shark's indigestion." Throwing Simon to the ground, he growled, "Get the plank."

Meanwhile the Princess Marie-Rose was growing accustomed to the sunlight. She looked around her at the crew of the bad ship *Torment* scurrying this way and that. And she saw Simon, standing brave and alone, with his hands tied, and although she pitied the young man, she hadn't the faintest clue who he was.

Simon was thrust on to the plank. The sharks circled hungrily beneath. The sea was dark and choppy.

"Walk!" growled Razelbreath.

Simon took a step forward. He looked at the sea, he looked at the sky and finally he looked back at the beautiful Princess Marie-Rose.

He cried out, "I have a last request."

Razelbreath sighed.

"Okay. But make it snappy."

Simon took a deep breath. "I would like a syrupy treacle and cinnamon pudding."

"Denied," said Razelbreath. "Get on with your stroll."

"Very well," said Simon, taking another step, "I would like a boat made of chocolate chip and coconut ice-cream."

"To sail away in, I suppose?" laughed Razelbreath cruelly. "Don't waste my time, I'm getting hungry."

Simon took a final step, and cried, "I would like a cake made of snow white cream, tasting of lemon and heaven."

"Please Captain Razelbreath, save him!" cried the voice of Marie-Rose. "I will marry you gladly, only save his life – for I love him."

But the wicked Captain Razelbreath only replied, "Croak!"

For he had turned that instant into a small and insignificant toad, destined to be ignored forevermore.

There was a wedding feast on the *Torment* that day – it was for Simon and the Princess Marie-Rose. Simon cooked the most amazing feast and the sailors were quite happy to accept him as their new captain – they had never liked the old one.

And the new captain's skill as a chef spread far and wide: ships for miles around came to sample the excellent cuisine on board the good ship *Torment*. The crew made wonderful waiters. Even the sharks still hung around because the scraps were so tasty.

As for Razelbreath the Toad, he lived in a tiny cage

on the deck, and was fed tiny, beautiful meals which he would gobble up in one mouthful and then croak for attention, which he never received.

And Captain Simon and the Princess Marie-Rose lived a long and peaceful life. Well, as peaceful as you can get, on the wicked high seas.

SARA CONKEY

Sara Conkey was born and lives in Birmingham. She first worked as a researcher for a children's independent TV company, and is now a BBC radio producer. She has had some children's poetry published, but this is her first piece of children's fiction. Her hobby is eating chocolate.

She says: "To write for children is to write for an audience that is unforgiving. They won't tolerate being bored and they can sniff out pretension at 500 paces. They know that play and imagination are vital to life. With adult fiction, you can be slick and intellectual and they'll be impressed. With children, they'll simply find a kite to fly instead."

Runner-up

A Mouthful of Gold

Sean Taylor

Illustrated by
Chris Fisher

The farmhouse door flew open, and an old man tumbled out.

"Get lost! You miserable, mollycoddled, mop-headed MOANING MINNIE!"

The old man picked himself up and shrugged at me and my dad.

"All I asked them for was a pint of milk!" he said. "You watch out for those two. Ali and Obi are the most bad-tempered brothers you ever met. They own this big farm and all the goats for miles around, but they won't do anyone a favour."

"We know," said my dad. "But it's carnival day. We have to ask them for a goat."

Once a year at the carnival, a goat was made Queen of our village. She was crowned with a feathered hat, and for one day she could do whatever she wanted: eat the best tomatoes from the market, wander into people's kitchens. Nobody would shoo her away – even if she climbed into their bed and went to sleep!

The old man wished us good luck, and walked off down the dusty road. We knocked, and the door burst open again.

"Yes!"

"Excuse us, Ali," said my father. "But it's carnival day."

"So what?"

"We need a Goat Queen for the day. But you and your brothers have all the goats."

Ali's brother Obi appeared in the doorway.

"They want a goat, do they?"

"Just to borrow," I said.

"Borrow a goat! BORROW A GOAT! What do you think this is – a library for lending animals? Geddoutofit you nose-picking, namby-pamby, nappy-brained NINCOMPOOPS!"

We were sent away empty-handed. Without the Goat Queen, that year's carnival was nothing worth remembering. But one day I found out what happened to those brothers *after* we left. And that is a story you will never forget.

After sending us away, Ali and Obi went down to their barn. There in the hay, wobbling on rubbery legs, was a beautiful new-born goat. Her fur was as brown as coffee and her eyes were as bright as two summer stars.

"Another one to feed," grumbled Obi. "Catch her and put her in the pen."

"Why should I catch her?" muttered Ali. "You catch her you lousy, lazy, lumbering LAUNDRY-BASKET!"

"LAUNDRY-BASKET? What about you – you . . . pernickety, pumpkin-bummed, poker-faced, PLONKER! You catch her."

The shouting made the baby goat bleat, and both brothers caught sight of something very strange. There was a golden glint in her mouth.

"Oi!" said Obi. "What's that?"

He touched a finger against the goat's lips.

"Hey. Open your mouth," he muttered, prodding her. "What's that inside? EH? Open your mouth, you snotty little goat!"

She bit his finger. Obi snatched away his hand with a yell. The goat stared back. Her lips were sealed.

"Open your mouth!" said Ali, picking up a fork. "Or I'll knock you into the middle of next week!"

The goat stood still.

Ali swung the fork at her. He missed and hit Obi's arm. Obi's arm hit a shelf. The shelf wobbled. A milk-churn toppled on to Ali's head. Ali stumbled into a haystack. The haystack collapsed over Obi. And the little goat smiled.

"Look," said Obi, shaking hay out of his hair. "Look."

Ali sat up. There in front of him was a smiling goat with a perfect set of gold teeth.

"A MOUTHFUL OF GOLD!" said Ali.

"She must be worth a fortune," said Obi.

"Let's take her to the city," whispered Ali. "We'll be rich."

For once the brothers agreed with each other. So the next day they set off for the city, dragging the goat behind them on a chain.

Neither of them had ever been to the city before. The streets were full of angry cars and clattering feet. Everyone was in too much of a fluster to give a second glance to two dusty farmers and a goat. Ali and Obi wandered until it was dark, then went to sleep in the doorway of a greengrocer's shop.

They were woken by an old woman.

"Oi! I've got to open my shop," she grumbled, wiping her hands on her apron. "What are you doing in my doorway with a goat?"

"We're going to make our fortune," said Obi proudly.

"And how do you intend doing that?"

"By selling this goat," said Ali.

"That scrawny thing!" laughed the greengrocer. "I wouldn't give you a bag of cabbage tops for that!"

But just then the goat yawned, showing every one of her glistening golden teeth. The grocer gasped.

"Look at that!" she said. "A gob full of gold."

The brothers told her their story and she was so amazed that she invited them in.

"Look," she said. "You're right. People will be interested in this goat. So what if I offer you my back room and put a notice in the window saying there's a miracle upstairs? People will come in to see, and maybe I'll sell them something on their way out."

The brothers had imagined something a bit more exciting than a greengrocer's back room. But it was better than sleeping in the street, so they carried the struggling goat upstairs and chained her down.

The grocer was right. First her regular customers went up to see the goat. Then a reporter came, and her photograph appeared in the local newspaper. Soon people were queueing round the block to visit the little grocery.

Everyone was happy, except the baby goat. She hated showing her teeth to the visitors, and wriggled and tugged at the end of her chain until her neck was red and raw.

A week after the brothers arrived in the city, a very long car drew up, and out got a huge man with a pudgy grey face.

"Good morning," he said. "Mr Copperdopolis is my name. I run the largest jewellery shop in the city. I hear you have a goat with gold teeth."

"We do," said the greengrocer. "Step this way."

Upstairs Mr Copperdopolis gripped the goat tightly with his soft, fat hands. He peeled back her lips like he was skinning a tomato. He stared coldly into her mouth through a shiny eye-glass. He tapped at her gums with a silver hammer, and dumped her back down.

"These teeth are genuine gold," he said. "Gentlemen, I can make you rich."

"How?" asked Ali.

"Well," said Mr Copperdopolis, rubbing two

chubby fingers against the tip of his pale nose, "you kill the goat and bring me the teeth. I will make a necklace out of them. I shall tell people about this necklace in all the richest cities of the world. Then we will sell it to the highest bidder. And you two will never have to work again."

The brothers nodded.

"Think about it," said Mr Copperdopolis. "I will be back in three days to see what you have decided."

The next day an even longer car drew up, and out got a woman with sharp blue eyes, and short red hair.

"Good morning," she said. "Ms Spectrum from the City University of Science. I hear you have a goat with gold teeth."

The grocer showed her upstairs. She wriggled her fingers into rubber gloves and pulled out a set of pointed little knives and needles. The goat struggled and strained and scratched at the wall. Ms Spectrum jabbed her with a long needle and spent fifteen minutes prodding, probing and poking at her head.

"This is of great scientific significance," she said, looking up. "I can make you rich."

"How?" asked Obi.

"Well, give my scientists a year to experiment on

the animal in our laboratory. We will examine samples of skin, open the skull and cut out slices of the brain for analysis. Then, when we discover the cause of this condition, we will be able to produce *hundreds* of goats with gold teeth."

The brothers nodded.

"Think about it," said Ms Spectrum with a frosty smile. "I will come back in two days' time to see what you have decided."

The next day an even longer car drew up and out got a short, bearded man. His ears were jingly with dangling earrings. His wrists were spangly with glittering bangles. And there was a golden top-hat on his head. He was followed by a whole film crew, with lights, cameras, and make-up artists.

"Oh, my goodness," muttered the greengrocer. "It's Gavin Gold."

"Who?" asked Obi.

"He runs this TV show called *Gold is the Game*. He's crazy about anything gold."

"Good morning," said the little man, breezing into the shop. "Gold is the name. GOLD IS THE GAME!"

He paused as if waiting for everyone to clap.

"You've seen my quiz show? Yes? No? Well, we

used to have this monkey that juggled gold bananas. People got bored with it. I need something new. Something wacky. Something weird. This goat I've heard about could be the very thing."

Upstairs the little goat kicked and nipped until her whole body quivered. They powdered her nose, shone bright lights in her face and filmed her from every angle. Eventually Gavin Gold looked up and said,

"Boys. All that glitters is not gold . . . but this little mouthful is REAL. She is going to make *Gold is the Game* the most popular show on TV. She's cute. She's funny. She's going to feature on every show. We'll teach her to dance. If she can't dance we'll teach her to sing. If she can't sing we'll teach her to juggle!"

His little bearded face grew red with excitement.

"I'll be back tomorrow to make you an offer. Think it over boys. BIG MONEY!"

The brothers nodded and Gavin Gold scampered off with his film crew.

Ali and Obi wandered back downstairs, and before long they were arguing about which of the three offers to accept. The more they disagreed, the angrier they got. And the angrier they got, the louder they shouted. And the louder they shouted, the more they disagreed. So they never heard the great crash from upstairs, or the horrible squealing sound that followed.

It wasn't until the greengrocer screamed that they stopped their bickering and stumbled up the stairs to see what was happening. The grocer was stooped in the doorway of the back room, her face as pale as the moon.

"What is it?" said Obi.

"Robbers have broken in through the window. They've —"

"They stole her?"

"No. Look."

The robbers hadn't been able to steal the goat. The chain round her neck was too tight. She was still there — lying on her side trembling. She couldn't stand. Her eyes were as dim as two wet stones. And as she struggled to breathe, spots of dark blood trickled from her mouth. The robbers had pulled out her teeth.

The greengrocer unlocked the chain, reached down with one big gentle hand and spooned the goat up into her earthy old apron.

"Look to see if they took all her teeth," said Obi.

"Never mind the teeth," snapped the grocer, hurrying down the stairs. "She's dying. We have to get her to Mother Mooneye."

Mother Mooneye was very kind, very wise and *very magic*. She loved animals like no one else. And she was famous for being able to cure any sickness or injury an animal could have.

She lived in a room stashed from floor to ceiling with herbs and roots and bottles of medicine. When the grocer came knocking at her door she took the goat without a word, and waved her and the two brothers in.

She worked for one hour – straightening the goat's bones, bathing her wounds, and soothing her bruises. Then she looked up and said, "She'll be all right."

"But is there . . ." stammered Ali. "Do you . . . will she grow back her gold teeth?"

Mother Mooneye stared calmly back.

"I don't think there is anything we can do about that," she said.

"But I heard you could do anything for animals," grumbled Obi.

"I can," she replied.

"Well . . . just do something to get us the gold teeth

then," snapped Ali.

Mother Mooneye smiled.

"You really want these gold teeth, don't you?"

The brothers nodded.

"Well," she sighed, reaching up for a dusty yellow bottle, "there might just be a way. I don't know if it will work, but if you want to try, then why not? Each of you take a sip from this bottle and give the goat a kiss."

"Bluuuuuuurgh!" said Ali. "KISS A GOAT?"

"ON THE MOUTH?" asked Obi, screwing up his face.

"Yes. On the mouth. That's where the magic is."

"Trust her," said the greengrocer. "Mother Mooneye is always right."

So the brothers agreed. They wrinkled their noses and sipped from the bottle. Then they bent down with puckered lips and kissed the goat.

Nothing happened. They peered down at her mouth. Nothing.

"Useless!" said Obi, swinging round.

"If that's magic, I'm a goat myself!" shouted Ali.

The grocer gasped. Mother Mooneye smiled.

"I thought it might work," she said.

The brothers peered back down at the goat. It

didn't have gold teeth.

"Look in the mirror," whispered Mother Mooneye.

They looked up at the mirror and both snapped their big mouths shut.

"But . . ." said Obi. "We . . . you . . . it was . . ."

Ali slowly opened his mouth and peered inside.

"The goat was meant to have the gold teeth, not us!" he cried.

"Oh . . . she's better off without gold teeth," said Mother Mooneye. "I got the impression it was you who wanted them."

"Well it was," said Ali. "I mean it is."

"And now," she said, "you two are rich."

"She's right," said the greengrocer. "That jeweller will be back tomorrow. He'll buy your teeth from you, and think of the necklace he'll be able to make from two sets of gold teeth."

"No!" shouted Obi.

"And Ms Spectrum," whispered Ali. "If she sees our teeth she's going to want to open our skulls and cut out slices of our brains."

"No," whimpered Obi.

"And I hear Gavin Gold is interested too," said Mother Mooneye. "He's going to want you on every show. He'll teach you to dance, and if you can't dance he'll teach you to sing, and if you can't sing he'll teach you to juggle gold bananas."

"NO!" The brothers picked up the goat, and hurried away with their mouths very firmly closed.

Imagine when they returned to the village. They never shouted. They never argued. Wherever they went they kept their lips pulled tightly over their teeth. When carnival day came again, I went with my dad to ask them if we could borrow a goat. They just poked their heads round the door and nodded.

So we took a goat and crowned her with a feathered hat. She did whatever she wanted: ate the best tomatoes from the market, wandered into people's kitchens. She even climbed into someone's bed and went to sleep!

She was the happiest Goat Queen anyone could remember . . . even though she had no teeth.

SEAN TAYLOR

Sean Taylor lives and works in East London. He did a lot of different jobs, from teaching to spotwelding, before he joined Basement Writers in Tower Hamlets, where he discovered his love of writing. He is now a Writing Development Worker at Eastside Wordcentre, and a Literacy Tutor at Hackney Community College. He is also a writer in residence in schools in London's East End and has had his own poetry published, as well as editing two collections of poetry by young writers and adults.

He says: "I love writing and performing for children because I want them to know that writing is on their side. For a long time when I was young, writing and reading were chores. I associated them more with failure and pressure than fun. In my writing for children and my work with them, I just try to get them feeling that they can read and write for their own reasons. Reading and writing are not just about performing for teachers and parents; they are about freedom, sharing, exploring, making up your own rules if you want, and sorting things out too. They are about all kinds of success."

The Black Hole

Maggie Butt

Illustrated by
Valeria Petrone

For Amy and Katie

Everybody thinks it must be mega-thrilling to live on a space station. They say, "Ooh, how exciting, aren't you lucky children?"

But nothing could be further from the truth.

"How would you like it," I say, "if the nearest sweet shop was twenty light years in either direction?"

There's no nipping out for a comic when you're outside the earth's orbit, and, whatever the adverts say, I can promise you there's not a lot of chocolate in the Milky Way and none at all on Mars. Some kids think it must be brilliant not to have to go to school, but I soon put them right.

"No school," I tell them, "equals no friends, no parties, no sleepovers, no putting on shows. Nobody to play with except my kid brother."

One glance at my brother Mort, with his socks

round his ankles and a vacant look on his face, tells them they wouldn't fancy that. But it's hardly surprising he looks bored, because I have to tell you, life is fairly bleak up here.

Don't get me wrong, we have absolutely everything we need. But nothing we want. Nowhere to ride bikes or go swimming or fly kites. And they only let us use the Reality Helmet at weekends. They say it'll give us square eyes, but we know that's an old astronaut's tale.

There's only two things to break the monotony of growing up on a space station. My favourite pastime is teasing Mort till he flies into a rage – although lately even that's getting a bit dull.

The other is pocket money day.

You may not think that's much to get excited about, if you have to earn your pocket money by cleaning the car or tidying your room or taking out the rubbish. But we don't have a car, and my room gets tidied by a house-bot and the rubbish is all recycled and made into clothes for us. (The nearest Marks-and-Spencerama is two planets away.)

So we earn our pocket money by fishing. Not in water of course, because that's rationed up here. (Actually, I forgot to mention, that is one of the only good things about space stations – we don't have our hair washed very often.)

No, what we fish in is the Black Hole.

Of course, you can imagine, when the Black Hole first opened up in the living-room floor, the grown-ups wouldn't let us anywhere near it. First of all they wanted to study it and said we got in the way. Then, when they'd probed it and sampled it and found out everything about it, they said we had to stay away in case we fell into it and got turned into anti-matter. As if we'd be so stupid. But we kept nagging and so in the end they put these railings round it and said we could go fishing as long as we showed them everything we caught. After that, they had a discussion and decided that as we obviously couldn't be trusted, they'd make sure we showed them everything by paying us for what we reeled in. But maybe I'm going too fast – perhaps you didn't realize there was lots of stuff flying around in space.

Haven't you ever wondered what happens to all the things you lose? They never turn up in the Lost Property cupboard, do they? That's because they're all spinning round and round in space, like washing in a huge tumble-dryer. And so we earn our pocket money by fishing around in a kind of lost-property soup. We use super-telescopic Meganets and what we find is basically all the stuff you lose.

So, for instance, we fish out loads of single gloves and hair-elastics and Biros. Our mum and dad only pay us about 10 Krions each for those because there's so many of them. Still, they're useful for the recycling. They turn out some fabutrendsome clothes.

What's interesting is we never know which things the adults are going to pay most for. Once my brother fished out a crocus and they nearly went crazy. Grown men wept and spouted poetry and all the adults went without sleep and spent hours in the labs till they found a way of encapsulating it in plastic to keep forever. I know flowers are pretty unusual, but I still think 1,000 Krions was a lot to pay for it. It was decent of Mort to split the money with me, though. Now we've both got enough for the Swimerama next time we land somewhere. If we ever do.

Anyway, I wouldn't have paid that much for a crocus. The thing I'd have paid 1,000 Krions for is the doG. The grown-ups thought it was only worth 40 Krions, if you can believe that, but at least they did let us keep it after it had been debacterialized.

I couldn't believe my eyes when I fished it out – a

real doG. I'd only ever seen one on the screen before. You've probably never seen one – in fact, you probably think it's just a spelling mistake, but it isn't. It's a bit like an earth canine to look at, but that's where the similarity ends. This is a doG with a capital G. It can do anything that starts with the letter G. Do G. Get it?

Years ago, when the first doG was discovered, they didn't realize to begin with that there was anything special about it. It could Growl and Gnash you see, it could Gnaw at bones and Guzzle its food like any ordinary dog.

But then came night and it started to Glow, to Gleam, to Glitter and to Glint. The kids thought it was brilliant. No more torches. No more night-lights. Just keep your doG on the end of your bunk. But the grown-ups panicked, just like you'd expect, and whisked it off to test for radioactivity and such-like.

The tests took months before some brain-box hit on the truth. There was nothing dangerous about this animal, it just happened to be able to do anything beginning with G.

Not the nouns. You can't *do* a gangster or a greyhound or a guinea-pig or gymkhana.

It could only do the verbs, the doing words. To

Guard, to Gallop, to Grab, to Gaze, to Glance and so on. It could do G. That's when they named it. But they still wouldn't let the kids have it to play with. Not until they'd run through the Universal Megadictionary to make sure there weren't any harmful-to-children words beginning with G. And finally, when they'd checked and double-checked every single word they finally pronounced doGs safe to keep as pets.

The Interplanetary Rule Book says that pets aren't allowed on space stations, so until I fished out this doG, we didn't have any animals. We thought they might not let us keep him, but I guess they know it's a bit boring for us sometimes, so as I say, they let him stay. Which is just as well really.

Having the doG around really changed everything. Mort liked to get him to Gargle, and I must admit it's pretty hard not to join in yourself when he starts to Giggle.

I liked to sit down with him at night when he was Glowing comfortingly and have a lovely, chummy Gossip.

Or if I was in a bad mood, it was great to have someone who would join in a good old Glower and Grumble and Grimace. The Grimacing pulled his face into such strange expressions that it usually made me start to smile and then the doG would start to Grin and finally we'd both end up in a heap of Giggles. That was megabrill – almost as good as having a real friend.

Having the doG was far better than teasing Mort. In fact I'd almost stopped that completely, except when he wasn't expecting it, just to keep in practice. I told him I'd grown out of it. And even pocket-money day didn't seem so exciting but still, there was always the chance we might fish out something just as good as the doG, and we were still saving for our next planet-leave. So last Saturday, off we went with our Meganets and our packed lunch to sit by the Black Hole.

For the first half-hour it was much as usual. I got a baby's sock, Mort got a red glove with a hole in one finger, I got a broken pencil. Then I got a real find – a love letter. As soon as I realized what it was, I started to read it out to Mort in my best soppy-teenager voice: "I long for you my darling every hour." Mort clutched his heart and staggered about pitifully. And the doG Gazed longingly and Gesticulated (waved his paws about) romantically at appropriate moments.

Well, we were all so busy laughing at the letter that we forgot Mort had left his meganet trailing in the hole.

Suddenly the doG stiffened and stood still. We stopped too, and listened. Slowly we became aware of the weirdest sound you have ever heard. It started like thunder a long way off and grew louder and deeper until everything in the room began to shake. It was low and mournful and terrifying and it seemed to be coming from the hole.

"Pull the net in," I shouted. "Quick."

The doG was there first. He Grabbed the net, and we quickly got behind him and pulled.

"It's too heavy," cried Mort. "We've caught something huge."

"Let go," I yelled, over the thunderous rumblings. By now every bone in my body was vibrating, like being at a rock concert.

We all let go at once and tried to protect our ears. The net fell away and for a second we thought we were safe.

But the sound was still getting louder and then, through the hole, appeared the pointed ears and the wing-tips of a horrible Something.

It was hard to make out its shape because it was as

black as the hole itself, with great, flapping umbrella-like wings. As it emerged from the shadows, we could see its mouth was open and the deafening sound was pouring out, rolling round the room and crashing into our ears. Mort fell to the ground, holding his ears while the giant dragon-bat slowly circled the room above us watching us hungrily with its glowing red eyes.

I ran to comfort Mort, bending low and keeping my ears covered as best I could. And then, out of the corner of my eye, I saw the doG move to the centre of the room. He began to pirouette like a ballerina, to twirl, to whirl, to spin, to rotate. In short, to Gyrate. The monster fixed him with its terrible fiery eyes. The awful moaning sound began to die away. The dragon-bat hovered above us and now we were all watching the doG as the spinning turned into amazing Gymnastics.

He did flik-flaks back across the room, gathering momentum and then cartwheeled with amazing speed towards the monster. He Glittered as he spun, like a huge Catherine wheel. And with the last cartwheel he flew into the air towards the astonished and now silently hovering monster. The doG hit the monster a glancing blow in his enormous belly and it

fell to the floor, winded. The doG bounced hard on its wobbling stomach and Grappled with it like a wrestler for a few seconds. I held my breath. Mort could only bear to peep between his fingers.

Then the door flew open and the adults rushed in, and all bumped into each other as they stopped like statues in the doorway. Mum pushed past to get to me and Mort and took us in her arms. The others took aim at the monster, but didn't dare to fire in case they hurt the doG.

Then, "What on earth?" and "What the blue blazes?" they cried, for something wonderful was happening.

Everywhere the doG had touched the monster he left a silver coating, which was spreading all over the hideous black body. As it spread, it petrified the monster like a giant carving till at last it lay there, silver and motionless, its great tummy like a shining hill.

The doG stepped back.

The scientists stepped forward.

"What is it?" "What's happened?" they asked each other.

"It looks like zinc," said Mum. "Do you know what − I think he's Galvanized the monster, coated him in zinc!"

The doG began to Giggle proudly next to me and I gave him my biggest hug. "You're the best pet in the universe," I told him. "You've saved all our lives."

The scientists moved in around the beast. "What is it?" they asked.

"I think I know," I said. They all turned to me. "I think it was a nightmare that someone lost a long time ago when the Universe was new."

They nodded wisely and agreed. "It jolly well looks like one. Clever girl." Then they rubbed their hands together. "We'd better do some tests," they said gleefully.

Mum and Dad gently gathered us all up and took us away from the living room and the silver monster.

"No more fishing in black holes for you," said Dad.

"And no more living on space stations," said Mum.

Dad looked at her questioningly, but she shook her head. "No, I've made up my mind," she said. "We're going to find a nice little planet with parks and lakes and a nice quiet school for the children to go to —"

We never heard what else she said because Mort and I were whooping with joy and dancing a jig and the doG was Galloping around and Glowing and Giggling until we all collapsed in a happy heap.

And if it's your planet and your school I come to, I promise you two things – I'll never say it was boring living on a space station and if you phone after dark and tell me you're scared, I'll come straight over and we'll sleep with the doG Glowing comfortingly on the end of our beds all night long.

MAGGIE BUTT

Maggie Butt lives in North London with her husband Tim and two daughters, Amy (aged nine) and Katie (aged six). After taking an English degree, she worked as a newspaper reporter and a BBC TV documentary producer, and she now lectures at Middlesex University in writing for journalism, radio and the screen. Although she has written professionally for newspapers and television, The Black Hole is her first published story for children. She is currently working on a children's picture book text and a radio play.

She says: "This was my first story for children and I found it wonderfully liberating to write because the only boundaries were the creaking limits of my own imagination. The Black Hole was actually inspired by a dream my daughter Amy related to me – a glimpse into the brilliantly visual and funny and bizarre imagination of a child. I think the best children's books tap into all that and it's certainly exciting to try and make a direct connection with such richness through language. It is also vitally important that we continue to make that link, so our children will learn to love books and also to value their own imaginative and creative powers."

The Knight Who Lost His Marbles

Charles Lowndes

Illustrated by
Angela Brooksbank

To Sharony Zid *(the Colourful Wall)*,
the children's radio station in Sarajevo.

It was warm indoors. Mother had soup bubbling on the stove. I had been working in the fields all afternoon, and it had been getting steadily colder as the wind grew stronger. We sat on the bench in the corner, enjoying the warmth. The strangers were talking to our parents, making them laugh. Their saddlebags had strange designs in the leather, twisting leaves, animals we'd never seen before, writing we couldn't read.

I'd seen them first. I was emptying my basket of stones at the top end of Long Field. Two strangers on tired horses, coming over West Hill, coming from nowhere. Even Father couldn't remember anyone coming from beyond West Hill.

The tall one had a long face. Although he was obviously not a servant, because of the rich cloth and strange colours in his cloak, he was very respectful to the short one. He had a round face with a short red beard and his eyes were always smiling.

It is not polite to ask a traveller too much about his business, and Mother and Father are always polite, but I think they were just as bursting to know as we were. The strangers cheerfully accepted the offers of food and shelter and were now talking about the care of horses. Father could talk about horses all night, and it looked as though he was going to, when he mentioned the problems of keeping our animals in the barns when the Dragon was about, and how this meant that we had to be very careful with the storing of the hay, and how he'd taught us all to make a decent stook as soon as we were old enough to walk into the meadows – when the short one said, "Stop!"

We all shuffled in amazement on our bench, because we knew it wasn't polite to say, "Stop!" like that, and we wondered how Father would react.

But the short stranger smiled with his mouth as well as his eyes, and made a gesture with his hands and asked Father to forgive him, but would he mind just explaining in a little more detail about the Dragon?

So Father did, and we realized that these two came

from some strange place where there was no Dragon. They looked at one another as though they were trying to work out if Father was making it up, but of course Father doesn't make things up except to make Mother laugh, and by this time she was busy ladling out the soup.

The short stranger said it sounded worse than the taxes levied by the worst kind of tyrant, and he knew a thing or two about the worst kind of tyrant – at which the tall one put a hand on his arm as if to stop him saying too much. It worked, because the short one stopped talking about tyrants and asked more about the dragon, and had anyone tried to get rid of it.

Father had his soup in front of him by this time, and he likes his soup, so Mother explained about the valiant knights who'd tried to get rid of the Dragon, and how they'd died in mortal combat, and how the king had said that enough was enough and although he didn't want to stop anyone being brave, the court was getting so empty and there were so many widows to look after that no more knights could challenge the dragon. We farmers would just have to live with the lost animals and burnt haystacks and harvest suppers ruined by the noise and smell.

And as the farming in our valley is good, and the winters not always too bad, and the fishing is wonderful, well, we thought the king was probably right. All the same, Father would go very quiet when the Dragon had been, because the Dragon always seemed to take the best lambs, and set fire to things at the worst time. And my brothers and I sometimes had dreams where we killed the Dragon, but we had not very nice dreams where the Dragon killed us and we woke up and we were unhappy and cold in the dark and too frightened to move. So we all wanted rid of the Dragon, but nobody knew how.

When Mother had explained all this there was silence for a while, except for the house noises: the fire, the creak in the roof beam over the larder, an occasional mouse scuttering in the ceiling.

Then the short stranger said a few sentences in some strange language to the tall one, who shook his head and seemed to be disagreeing. They argued for a while, and the short one must have won, because the tall, respectful man eventually nodded his head and then stayed quiet.

There was another silence, and then the short stranger spoke.

"Please forgive my discourtesy in speaking to my

steward in our own language. I should perhaps have explained earlier that I am a knight in our own country; but we have travelled far, by secret and lonely routes and have had the habit of keeping the burden of our story to ourselves. It is a long one, and we shall not trouble you with it, except to say that the burden of tyranny can be worse than that of dragons. Nonetheless, we fought and lost against the scourge of our people, and had to flee by night, carrying only what you see. Our families are in hiding, our lands have been seized, and our friends have been turned against us by lies and threats.

"As we have been unable to protect our own, we have little to lose and all to gain by pitting our wits against this creature, this Dragon, which preys upon your handsome, hospitable country. I am not subject to your king, so it is with no disrespect that I may challenge your Dragon."

Mother started to protest; we all sat on the edge of the bench, forgetting to clean out our soup bowl with the bread; two mice scuttered all the way across the ceiling from one side of the room to the other. But Father said, "You are a brave man, my lord, but courage may not be enough against the Dragon."

"Courage was not enough in our struggle, friend

farmer. We have learnt some dark and cunning ways, studied magic and medicines that harm as well as heal, and set tricks and traps that caused us shame, but saved our lives. We have learnt that the front gate is not always the best way in, that the honour of an open challenge is not always as useful as the silent approach by night, that an enemy with greater numbers may be greatly confused if he can be tempted into too small a place. We have learned above all that knowing the enemy is a better weapon than the sharpest blade. So come, friend, tell us everything about this Dragon who steals your sheep and fires your fodder."

At this point Mother shooed us all off to bed and there was a great deal of grumbling from us and clucking from her and eventually three words from Father, so up we went, rather quietly.

But once we were all in the bed, I could hear Father's voice as he told all the Dragon tales he knew, which takes a long time, and he was still only on his father's father's time when I found I wasn't listening any more and suddenly it was morning.

By the time I'd splashed water on my face from the well in the yard, and snapped off a hazel twig to clean my teeth with, the two strangers were at their porridge. The tall one, the steward as we now knew, was flushed and sneezing, and the knight was telling him to stay behind.

"But – *achoo!* – someone will need to hold the horses and stand lookout."

Although I knew it wasn't polite to join in a grown-up conversation without being asked, I blurted out, "I'll be the lookout and hold the horses."

Before Mother and Father could say anything, the knight's gaze fell on me. His eyes were still smiling, as always, but his mouth was serious. "You're a good lad, and I've seen that you can keep quiet. A lookout needs to be quiet. Can you whistle like a blackbird?"

I whistled, first like a male and then like a female blackbird. He laughed. He turned to Father and said, "You know the plan. There's risk, as there always is in these matters, but if things go badly for me he'll be able to bring back the news. And if things go well, he'll share in the glory. May I borrow your son?"

Mother started to speak, then stopped, and concentrated very hard on the porridge. Father looked at me, and then he looked at the knight. "Yes," he said. "But I need him back."

The knight said in a very serious voice that he heard what Father said.

And that's how I came to witness what happened.

It took us almost all day to reach Dragon Mountain, because the knight said we ought to go round by the north. He didn't say much as we rode, and I concentrated on practising keeping quiet. We ate Mother's oat cakes and the bacon by a stream some time after noon, but he still didn't say much. Then he told me a bit about the plan, and I began to understand.

Dragon Mountain was a terrible place: it smelled dragony, and the trees were mostly burned. There were no birds, and the few streams we crossed had black water, and a few muddy reeds. It was cold. The Dragon would be sleeping, of course, because it was daytime and still a week and a half before full moon.

We dismounted about half a mile from Dragon's Lair Mouth. There were sheep bones lying around in front of the cave, and the smell was very strong. It got into your throat as well as your nose. There were some rocks and the stump of a silver birch, and the knight told me to wait there. I was to keep watch for anything untoward, and whistle like a blackbird unless it was immediate danger, when I should shout. If his plan failed, then I was to keep silence and ride hard back to the farm, leading the knight's horse.

The knight left his sword, because he said that even the finest steel was no good against dragons. Only cunning could work, cunning mixed with knowledge. He smiled at me with his whole face, and walked away to Dragon's Lair Mouth.

When he was about a stone's throw away, he stopped, and sat on a rock, after brushing off the sheep bones, and making some other preparations.

Then he pulled out a small trumpet from under his cloak, and began to blow short, discordant blasts. He called out: "Dragon! You smell worse than a drain in midsummer. Your breath could curdle milk. You stink like a rabid rat's armpit!"

I knew I was supposed to keep lookout, but I couldn't keep from watching the mouth of the cave, to see what happened next.

"Dragon!" shouted the knight, in an even louder voice. "I've never known such an appalling smell. Even when a hedgehog died in the water-butt and decomposed, there wasn't such a smell. You are . . . revolting!"

The silence that followed was suddenly broken by a roaring noise, like a waterfall suddenly coming over a cliff. The Dragon was awake! And there was a noise behind me! But it was only one of the horses fidgeting. I looked back to the cave mouth – and there was the Dragon. At least, I could see smoke, and two glittering points of light through the smoke: the Dragon's eyes.

"Oh, so you're awake, you putrid tub of donkey's dos. You're more disgusting than a guinea fowl's gizzard, even more obnoxious than a baboon's behind."

The Dragon must have lost his temper at this point, because he came rushing out of the cave, spouting flame and roaring with rage. This was the critical moment in the knight's plan. For a moment I thought it had failed, that the knight would be killed, and I would have to ride back alone. But then – then the Dragon went sliding and skidding forwards, tripped, his tail caught on a rock, his great scaly body arched upwards, and he turned a huge clumsy somersault. His scaly body ended up bending in half. He landed CRASH on his face – the flames from his nose setting light to the scales of his tail, which made him bellow even louder.

The knight was sheltering behind the rock, laughing with relief and delight. It had been a simple trap: a bag full of glass marbles, scattered in the Dragon's path. The oldest trick of all for dealing

with bullies – make them angry enough to lose control, and then trip them up.

The Dragon was whimpering with pain, trying to lick his scorched tail, but there were still flames coming out of his nose, so it only made things worse. With an enormous effort, he straightened himself out, staggered a few feet, took off, and flew away in terrible embarrassment and considerable pain. He was no longer in charge, and couldn't bear the humiliation. We never saw him again.

That night Father let me drink beer for the first time, and Mother cooked two whole salmon in pastry. My brothers ate a whole cake between them. There was a stream of visitors coming in and out to hear the news, and then rushing to tell their friends.

The knight and his steward left the next day, but people had already started singing songs about them. After they'd gone, we found they'd left various pieces of luggage behind: Mother found a beautiful gold necklace in a tattered velvet bag behind her oatmeal tub, and when I went to bed that night I found the bag of marbles had fallen down inside my slippers.

Years later, when I was grown up and had children of my own, I heard that a certain knight, who'd been forced into exile by a cruel king, had travelled abroad where he and his steward had many adventures before returning home, and leading a successful rebellion which set his country free.

The knight, they said, had been to a beautiful country and killed a dragon with one blow of a mighty sword.

But I knew better, because I was there, and I saw what really happened. I wonder if he ever realized he lost his marbles at our house, after he tricked the Dragon.

CHARLES LOWNDES

Charles Lowndes lives in West London, and was educated at Oxford and the Open University. Since graduating, he has worked for the British Forces Broadcasting Service, a 24-hour radio service for the Forces and their families around the world, and he is currently the Controller of Programmes. His hobbies are walking and sailing. Although he's written stories for broadcast, this is his first published piece of work. He and his wife Lesley have three sons aged fifteen, thirteen and ten.

He says: "There were many books in our house. Then there were stories from my mother, who was brought up in Burma where there were elephants; stories on the radio, where there were elephants and dragons; and visits to the library in Kendal, which meant driving over the fells, where there were sheep. On my father's shelves were the Andrew Lang Fairy Tales, in all their magical colours. And there was Miss Benn's Bookshop. Miss Benn had read all the books there are, and knew in which order you should read the stories. I expect that's why I like books and stories."

The Tug of War

GRAHAM LAURENCE

Illustrated by
ANT PARKER

For Sophie

Everyone in the whole wide world has got a best friend and Floyd the chicken's best friend is Nick the duck. Nick and Floyd like each other so much they can't bear to be apart for more than a couple of hours at a time. They live next door to each other in the big new block of flats by the park and they work at the same car factory over by the station. They even go to the same dentist.

Last Friday evening Nick and Floyd were down at the gym as usual when Floyd spotted a large colourful poster on the wall by the chest expanders. It was advertising a tug of war competition which was going to be held at the park a week on Saturday. Floyd had never heard of a tug of war, but there was a picture of some chickens and ducks pulling a thick rope and underneath that there was a place to write your name if you wanted to take part. How exciting! thought Floyd and he rushed off to tell Nick all about it. Nick didn't know what a tug of war was either but when Floyd showed him the poster he noticed something Floyd had missed.

"What's on the other end of the rope?" said Nick. Floyd looked. Nick was right, you couldn't see what was on the other end of the rope because the picture wasn't big enough. The rope just ended in mid-air where the picture finished at the edge of the poster.

"It looks as though it could be a bit difficult to me," said Nick.

"Whatever it is," said Floyd, "it can't possibly be harder than doing fifty push-ups on your beak."

Nick and Floyd wrote their names at the top of the list of entrants and went back to their exercises.

On Monday morning Nick and Floyd were back at work at the car factory. Nick's job was to put the doors on and Floyd was in charge of pumping the tyres up. All weekend they had been talking about the tug of war competition and they had decided that they needed to get some more help in case it turned out there was something really big on the other end of the rope.

When lunchtime came they told all their friends at the factory about it and after work everyone went down to the gym. They all crowded around in the corner by the skipping ropes trying to get a good look at the poster but still no one had a clue what a tug of war could be. On closer inspection everyone agreed on one thing. Whatever was on the end of the rope was something very big and very heavy because the rope in the picture was so thick and because there were six chickens and ducks all pulling as hard as they could.

The only thing that anyone could think of as big and heavy as that was a chest of drawers, and the only person that had one was Nigel the chicken.

"If," said Floyd, "we are going to have to pull Nigel's chest of drawers around the park on Saturday we had better start practising as soon as we can."

Everyone became very excited and there was a scramble to add names to the list of entrants. They all decided that the best place to practise pulling

Nigel's chest of drawers around on the end of a thick rope would be Nigel's back garden after work on Tuesday. Then Jeff the chicken managed to climb up on top of a box of tennis balls and said, "Three cheers for Nick and Floyd!" and everyone cheered loudly except for Nigel, who was beginning to wish he'd never come.

The next evening after work everybody squeezed into Nigel's back garden ready to start pulling his chest of drawers about. By this time almost half the factory had heard about the tug of war and nearly thirty ducks and chickens had turned up with bits and pieces of rope. Everyone wanted to be the first to tie their bit of rope to something and a couple of chickens had already begun pulling one of Nigel's deck chairs around the patio.

Nick and Floyd were inside the house with Nigel. They were trying to decide how they were going to get the chest of drawers out of Nigel's bedroom and into the garden. The problem was going to be getting it down the stairs. Suddenly Floyd had a brilliant idea.

"We can lower it into the garden through Nigel's

bedroom window," said Floyd. "That way we can get in some practice with the rope even before we've left the house!"

"That is very clever indeed," said Nick. Nigel wasn't sure.

Five minutes later, everything was ready. The thickest rope of all had been tied around the chest of drawers and Nick and a couple of big ducks were all set to tip it out of the window.

"Ready?" said Floyd.

"Ready," said Nick.

"Ready," said Nigel, and four of the strongest chickens who were holding the rope.

"Now," said Floyd.

Nick and the ducks let go of Nigel's chest of drawers and Floyd watched as it plummeted down to where a space had been cleared on the patio.

Smash! went the chest of drawers.

"Oh, dear," said Floyd. "The rope was too long."

Nigel dropped the rope and rushed to the window to see what had happened. All that was left of his chest of drawers was lots and lots of little bits of wood.

"Well, that was no good," said Floyd. "We should have carried it down the stairs after all."

"What are all those things blowing around outside?" said Nick, pointing into the garden.

Nigel looked.

"Oh, no!" he groaned. "I forgot to take everything out of the drawers first!"

All around the garden Nigel's underwear was stuck on bushes and hanging off branches, and one little chicken who had come with his daddy had tied his bit of rope to a pair of Nigel's pink boxer shorts and was busy pulling them around by the garage.

Back at the gym, Floyd was looking at the poster again when he suddenly realized he'd been wrong about the tug of war all along.

"The thing is," he said to Nick, who was on the rowing machine, "I don't think there's meant to be anything at all on the end of the rope in a tug of war."

Nick stopped rowing and got up to have a look.

"What is the point of having a rope if there's nothing on the end of it?" he said.

"I think," said Floyd, "that the idea of a tug of war is to keep the rope in the air by running backwards as fast as possible."

"Like a kite?" said Nick.

"Just like a kite," said Floyd.

"Floyd, you are very clever indeed," said Nick.

The next day after work everyone was back in Nigel's garden with their bits of rope. By now nearly everyone in the whole town had heard about Nick and Floyd's tug of war. When poor Nigel looked out of his bedroom window all he could see were lots of chickens and ducks squashed into his garden and a queue going twice around the house and down the High Street.

Nick got everyone's attention by banging on Nigel's dustbin lid and Floyd began to explain where they had gone wrong the day before. Jeff the chicken asked if Nigel was going to be throwing any more furniture out of his bedroom window and when Nigel said he wasn't about half the crowd went home.

Finally, it was time to start. Floyd got everyone to stand in a line holding the rope and said, "Ready, Steady, Go!"

Everyone ran backwards and pulled as hard as they could.

"Faster!" said Floyd "Faster!"

Two hours later Floyd said they could stop. It was no good. No matter how hard they all tried they couldn't get the rope off the ground. It was nearly time to pack up when Floyd had a brilliant idea. He took the rope and tied one end to Nigel's tree and got everyone to pull as hard as possible on the other end.

"See?" said Floyd. "It's working!"

Nick looked. Floyd was right, it was working. It was just like in the picture.

Two days later it was time for the competition. After all the practising they'd done with Nigel's tree everyone had become very good indeed at tug of war. The whole town was in the park to cheer them on and someone was even selling T-shirts with Nick and Floyd's faces on.

At exactly two o'clock an important-looking duck called Frank arrived to take charge. He was carrying the poster from the gym. Floyd introduced himself to Frank as the Team Captain and asked which tree they would be using.

"Pardon?" said Frank.

"I said," said Floyd, "which tree should we tie our rope to? If it's all the same to you I would like to use the big one by the swings."

"That isn't what happens in a tug of war," said Frank.

"Isn't it?" said Floyd.

"No," said Frank. Frank explained how to play tug of war properly. "The idea," said Frank, "is that you split up into two teams and each side pulls against the other."

"No trees?" said Floyd.

"No trees at all," said Frank.

"Oh," said Floyd. "What happens next?"

"What happens next," said Frank, "is that one team wins when the other is pulled across that line."

Frank pointed at a thick white line which had been painted on the grass just behind the spot where Nick was standing.

"Gosh," said Floyd. "This sounds even more exciting than playing tug of war with Nigel's tree!"

Once the rules had been sorted out Frank asked Floyd who the other team's captain was. Floyd said he didn't know. Frank unrolled the poster and had a look at the list of entrants.

"It's someone called Nick," he said.

"Oh, no, it can't be Nick," said Floyd. "You see he's my best friend so we've got to both be on the same side."

"Yes," agreed Nick.

Frank thought for a moment. "Well," he said, "you've both put your names at the top of the list where it says who the captains are."

Nick looked at the poster. Frank was right, they were both captains.

"Oh, dear," he said.

"Oh, no," said Floyd.

Everyone in the park went quiet.

"Well," said Floyd, "we'll just have to both be captains and do our best."

"Yes," said Nick, sadly.

Ten minutes later everything was ready. Nick and Floyd stood in the middle of the park facing each other, with their teams lined up behind them.

"Ready?" said Frank. Everyone picked up the rope.

"Steady?" said Frank. Everyone gripped it as firmly as they could.

"Go!"

Everyone pulled.

"Heave," said Nick to his team.

"Harder," said Floyd to his.

Backwards and forwards went the rope and the crowd cheered louder and louder.

"Pull more!" said Nick.

"Come on!" said Floyd, and everyone in the park started jumping up and down with excitement.

Suddenly, Jeff and Nigel both slipped over on the grass and Floyd's team lost their grip on the rope. Nick's team pulled faster and faster and harder and harder until they'd pulled Floyd's team right across the line. The crowd cheered like crazy and Frank shouted at the top of his voice, "The winners!" and gave Nick's team a big gold cup.

Nick said thank you to Frank and went to see how Floyd was. He found his friend sitting on the grass by the climbing frame, still holding on to one end of the rope.

"Well done," said Floyd, looking a bit disappointed.

"Well done to you as well," said Nick.

"Tug of war is a very good game indeed," said Floyd, and Nick agreed.

"It's a pity we couldn't be on the same side," said Nick.

"Yes," said Floyd, who was beginning to look a bit

happier, "but you know it doesn't really matter who won because we'll always be best friends."

"Yes," said Nick and they gave each other a big hug.

GRAHAM LAURENCE

Graham Laurence divides his time between Buckinghamshire and Chiswick. He studied economics in London and then attended a music college and went on to become a songwriter and composer. He likes reading, music and the cinema and is a member of the Marc Bolan Appreciation Society. This is his first published piece of fiction.

He says: "I am currently writing a novel which is going to blow everyone away in a year from now."

Making Friends

NORMA CLARKE

Illustrated by
JULIE ANDERSON

For Jake Judd

First I saw the swimming pool, then we heard the Shouty-Screamy family. That wasn't their real name of course. It was what Mum and Dad called them, under their breaths.

"Thank goodness our Jake isn't noisy like that," Mum said to Dad, giving one of her looks. We were all wearing sunhats, and shirts and shorts and new espadrilles.

We were on holiday. We'd had to drive all the way from the middle of England to the middle of Italy. A long way. And hot, which is why, when we got to the hotel, we went straight to the pool.

A small blond boy was running round and round the edge with an outsize water gun, squirting everybody and shrieking. A girl, much bigger and louder, chased him. A man was chasing the girl, making gorilla noises as he ran. And there was a woman with red hair and bright pink shoulders who was bouncing up and down on a sunbed and squeaking, "Oliver! Ogaboos! Here darling!"

That wasn't all. There was another boy hiding behind a tree and yelling at all of them.

"Oh, dear," my mum said. "What a shouty-screamy family."

So that's what we called them.

I stood by the poolside in my new swimming trunks (black, with a green stripe) and fiddled with my goggles. That was only for show. Really, I was getting a good look round. I felt very white and a bit scared. We didn't know anybody. I could hear strange-sounding languages all round me and the only people I could understand, sort of, were the Shouty-Screamies.

Mum said, "If you're not going in the water straight away, Jake, put some lotion on."

But I *was* going in the water straight away. I was going to do my dive. I learned to dive the week before we came away – at last! Till then, I was the only good swimmer in my class who couldn't dive.

"Go on then," Mum said.

"Don't watch me."

I stood with my toes over the edge. It was

wonderful to feel the sun stroking my shoulders, to be under a blue sky, to have cool blue water winking and blinking at my feet. I knew it would be like this, just like the picture in the travel agent's brochure. Heaven.

I raised my arms above my head, dreamily. Something brushed my leg, something soft and irritating, like a spider. I looked down. Then I saw it – a huge monster fly, with a talon like a rhinoceros's horn. And the talon was going inside my leg. I yelped. A split second later my leg was on fire. I leaped, swept the fly off, and fell with an almighty splash into the water.

When I came up, rubbing the water out of my eyes and rubbing the sore spot on my leg, the Shouty-Screamy girl was sitting on the steps, laughing at me.

"Horse flies," she said, in a merry voice. "They're everywhere. I hate them. They're disgusting. They're worse than my little brother."

"Your little brother?"

"Yes," she said, as if it were obvious. "He's everywhere, I hate him and he's disgusting. Did it bite you very hard?"

I lay on my back and let myself float a little away from her. I had a red sore and a bump as big as a tenpence across.

"Nasty," the girl said.

I didn't know what to say. I felt stupid.

"My name's Tatyana," she said. "What's yours? Have you just arrived? Is that car the only car you've got?"

Too many questions. I turned over and swam underwater to the other side. When I came back Tatyana was still there.

"Well?" she said cheerily.

"How old are you?" I asked her.

"Nine."

I thought she was going to say *twelve* at least. She was the same age as me.

"How many cars have you got then?" I said, trying to sound as if I didn't care one way or the other, which I didn't.

"Three."

"Three! You must be rich rich!"

She shook her head. She was sucking at a strand of hair on one side. "Daddy says we're very poor," she said sadly. "We may have to give up one of our houses."

"How many houses have you got?" I wasn't sure I really wanted to know, but I had to ask.

"Only two," she said, laughing.

I did a duck dive and swam a bit. When I came

back, Tatyana was still there, chewing her hair. "Does your mother have nerves?" she asked me, looking thoughtful.

"What are nerves?"

"Don't you know anything?"

"I know my leg hurts," I said. I was starting to wonder what sort of holiday I was going to have at this hotel. And I'd been looking forward to a holiday with a swimming pool for months and months.

To avoid the horse flies, you had to get up early. So that's what I did next morning.

You could still see the sore on my leg, but it didn't hurt. There was only one thing on my mind, and that was my dive. I woke up thinking about it.

I went down to the pool. Mum and Dad had a lie-in. Nobody was watching me and I didn't have to worry about horse flies, so I should have got my toes over the edge and my hands together over my head and bent my knees and lifted off so that I fell head first into the water. But I didn't.

I tried. It wouldn't come.

It took me a long time to get into the water at all. When I did, I bellyflopped just like I used to before I learned to dive.

I got out dripping and miserable. I ran back to the hotel and stood on our balcony making a puddle, and whined, "Mum! I've lost my dive."

"How can you lose your dive?" she said.

"I don't know. But I've lost it. It's gone."

She said (of course), "It'll come back."

"No it won't," I said, and threw myself on a sunbed.

"I hope you're not getting into one of your sulks," Dad said.

I didn't want to swim any more. I stayed on the balcony, secretly looking out for Tatyana and her brothers but they didn't come by. It was dead quiet. And hot. And boring.

Next day Mum said, "If you don't want to swim, let's go for a drive and visit some beautiful old hill towns."

I didn't want to do that, either. It was no fun cooped up in the back of the car, sweltering, getting sticky and headachy, while Mum and Dad oohed and aahed over geraniums on people's window-sills and pink bricks.

I didn't want to go round churches. I certainly didn't want to be dragged round art galleries. And I decided I didn't like Italian food.

"Can't we go home?" I said.

"Don't be silly," they said.

I was fed up. Next morning, the sun woke me again. Outside my bedroom window, the meadow and pine trees glowed.

I got up and slipped into my swimming trunks, put shorts and a sweater on top and slid on my espadrilles. There was humming in the air, and rustlings in the trees. In the sunlight it was already getting hot, but in the shadows it was bone cold. The grass was wet with dew.

I thought there'd be nobody else awake yet, but as I came round the outside of the games room I heard a tap-tap-tap sound.

I looked inside. It was the boy from behind the tree – Tatyana's brother, Benjie – playing table tennis on his own.

I took one look and turned away, but he called me back. "You can play if you like," he said.

I went to the table and picked up a chewed-looking bat. Benjie was one of those boys whose mouth hangs open, and who wears specs, and who always looks puzzled.

Benjie said, "My dad was playing with me but he got fed up. I'm not very good."

"Nor am I," I said, which was true because I'd

never played table tennis before. "Have you really got three cars and two houses?"

"I don't know," Benjie said, going for the ball.

"Do you like it here?" I asked, as the ball came towards me and I swiped at it and missed.

"Dunno."

Benjie wasn't keen on talking, nor was I, so we played ping-pong until he got fed up with me. Then we walked over to the pool and watched the men sweeping leaves off the surface with a huge rake.

"You can have breakfast at our table if you like," Benjie suddenly said.

I shook my head. "My mum and dad wouldn't like that."

"'Course they will," Benjie said. "You're on your own and there's three of us. There's not many other kids here. 'Course they'll want you to be friends with us."

"Will they?"

I never thought of that.

Then I heard a voice in my head. It was Tatyana's voice saying, *Don't you know anything?*

Perhaps I didn't want to have breakfast at their table. We only had one car and one house. My mum and dad only had one child. I was no good at ping-pong. I didn't like it here. I didn't like the food and – *and* – I'd lost my dive.

"Let's have a swim first," Benjie said.

"Race you," I said, stripping my clothes off. I could beat everybody in my class except Robert Randall.

"No," he said. "I can't swim properly. I only paddle."

I had to laugh. He said it so seriously and sounded so stupid.

"Do you wear a blow-up ring?" I asked. I couldn't help it.

"Sometimes."

"Don't you feel stupid?"

"It's better than drowning," Benjie said, getting into the water carefully and holding on to the side.

I jumped in with a glorious splash. It was cold. I swam quickly up to the other end and back.

"You're a good swimmer," Benjie said.

It was true, and he wasn't, so I didn't say anything.

"Can you dive?" he asked.

"Yes," I said.

"Show me."

"No."

Benjie didn't seem surprised I didn't want to dive.

He paddled up and down the shallow end of the pool, never letting go, but kicking his feet and splashing and having a good time. I did duck dives, and swam underwater.

"Go on," Benjie said after a bit. "Show me a dive. Just one."

"I don't feel like it," I said, very casually.

"I wish you would feel like it."

Some people were coming out of the hotel down to the pool. On the terrace, I could see the breakfast tables starting to fill up. Soon the horse flies would be out, spoiling everything.

What sort of day was it going to be? What did I feel like doing? Not going out in the car. Not sulking on the balcony with a boring book. Not wishing I was back home. What I felt like doing was diving and having breakfast with the Shouty-Screamy kids.

I got out of the water and stood, shivering and dripping, with my toes over the edge. I raised my arms above my head the way I'd learnt, and bent my knees.

"How do you do it?" Benjie asked. He was still in the pool, looking up at me and squinting in the sun.

"You bend your knees," I said. "You raise your arms and put your hands together over your head."

"And then?"

"And then you think about going into the water head first. You lift up and let your pointed hands guide you. You straighten your legs out behind and point your toes, if you can."

"Can you?" said Benjie.

"I'll try."

Below me was the water, blinking and tinkling. I thought hard about how I dived when I first got it right. I made a picture in my head. I imagined I was back in the swimming pool at home, and everything was familiar. Then I lifted off, kept my head down, and parted the water cleanly with my hands. My dive had come back.

I did a few more dives to be sure.

"I wish I could do that," Benjie said.

When I saw my dad stepping over for a quick swim before breakfast, I had to run up and tell him. "My dive came back! My dive came back!" And I showed him, and it hadn't gone away again.

So then I said, "Can I have breakfast on Benjie's table?"

He looked surprised, but he didn't let on that we'd been talking about them, and calling them names like Shouty-Screamy Family. So I went and

had breakfast with Benjie and found out that
Tatyana told stories, which *everyone* knew, and they
only had one car and one house.

"I was only trying to make friends," Tatyana said.

After breakfast we played in the meadow and then
we went to the pool. We filled up Oliver's outsize
water gun and took it in turns to run round the pool
shouting and screaming and squirting water at each
other.

"Can't you be friends quietly?" Mum said. I was
creeping up on Tatyana at the time, to push her in.
"It's no wonder their poor mother has bad nerves."

Tatyana let out an ear-piercing squeal as she went in
the water. Oliver crept up on me and pushed me in.

"I'll get you!" I yelled at the top of my voice.

Mum didn't like it, Dad didn't like it, most of the
people on holiday at the hotel probably didn't like it,
but we did.

Norma Clarke

Norma Clarke was born in London, and despite falling in love with the Lake District as a student at Lancaster University, now lives in North London. She has two teenage sons and since the early 1970s has been a part-time college lecturer, teaching literature to adults. Earlier this year she decided to stop teaching and go freelance as a full-time writer. Her first published work, an adult academic book, was published in 1990 and she has since had three children's books published.

She says: "Some people think if you write for children it's because you haven't grown up yourself. That may be so. But I think it's because children are wonderfully inventive and being around them always inspires me. They are generous but also severe readers. Only the best will do. Among my most satisfying moments as an author have been those times when I've been invited to a school to read my books to a class of eight or nine-year-olds, and they've laughed at the jokes."

The Princess in the Tower Block

FINBAR O'CONNOR

Illustrated by
SUE HEAP

To my wife, Margaret Levey

There was once a princess who was tired of being in fairy tales. She was sick of getting locked up in towers by ugly witches and rescued by princes in ridiculous tights. She wanted to stay out after midnight without finding that her carriage had turned into a vegetable. And she had had enough of waking up every morning in a bed full of frogs claiming to be princes in disguise (most of the princes she knew looked like frogs in disguise anyway).

So one morning, while the king and queen were watching the princes playing leap-frog (or the frogs playing leap-prince – it was sometimes hard to tell) the princess took her magic mirror and ran away to the big city. She moved into an apartment on top of the tallest tower block in town because she was used to living in tall places and thought that this was why people called her Your Highness.

Now, as you know, all fairy-tale princesses have long golden hair which they have to brush for hours every morning. But our princess was bored with that so she went to a hairdresser and had her head shaved. Then she put on an old pair of jeans, a T-shirt and a pair of trainers and stood before her magic mirror.

"Mirror mirror on the wall," she said. "Who's the coolest of them all?"

And the mirror replied:

"You're dressed in rags – you look a fright!
You must have stayed out past midnight.
The handsome prince will be appalled, he
Will not want a wife who's baldy!"

"Who cares?" said the princess and went out on her balcony to look at the view.

"Coooeee!" called a distant voice. "Rapunzel, I'm home!"

Standing on the street far below, gazing adoringly up at her, was a prince in bright green tights.

"Oh, no," groaned the princess. "What do you want?"

"Rapunzel! Are you up there, my beloved?" he cried. "Let down thy golden locks that I might climb up and rescue thee!"

"Clear off, you smarmy git!" shrieked the princess.

The prince glared up at her.

"Loathsome hag!" he roared, shaking his fist. "Release my beloved Rapunzel of the golden hair or it'll be the worse for you!"

"I'm not a loathsome hag," said the princess crossly. "I'm a princess!"

"Forgive me, my beloved, I did not recognize thy baldy head," said the prince. "But now that the witch has cut off thy golden tresses how am I to scale yon lofty tower?"

"Do you have a ladder in your tights?" asked the princess sweetly.

"Well," replied the prince, "as a matter of fact I do."

"Then climb up that and see where it gets you!" she shrieked and stormed back indoors.

Just then the doorbell rang.

"Now what," sighed the princess as she answered it.

"Kissy kissy!" said a prince in yellow tights, taking her in his arms.

"Get off me, you slobbering oaf," cried the princess, struggling to escape.

"Wait a minute," said the prince as he let her go. "What are you doing up?"

"Why shouldn't I be up?" asked the princess.

"Because, Snow White," said the prince, "according to the seven dwarfs, your wicked stepmother gave you a poisoned apple that put you into an enchanted sleep. I'm supposed to kiss you and wake you up!"

"The seven dwarfs?" cried the princess in horror. "Don't tell me they're here too!"

"They were too busy down the mine I'm afraid," said the prince, handing her a bag of smelly socks. "But they sent along some washing."

"I'll give them washing!" shrieked the princess furiously.

"Keep your voice down," hissed a prince in purple tights, popping his head in the door. "You'll wake the Sleeping Beauty!"

"She's awake already," said Prince Yellowtights.

"I'm not surprised," said Prince Purpletights. "With Cinderella's ugly sister here yelling her head off!"

"How dare you," said the Princess. "I'll have you know I am nobody's ugly sister. I am a beautiful princess!"

"Well you could have fooled me, baldy!" said Prince Purpletights rudely. "Anyway, if you're really a beautiful princess, why aren't you asleep?"

"Wait a minute," said Prince Yellowtights. "Maybe

she couldn't sleep because of the pea."

"Pee?" spluttered the princess. "What pee?"

"In the bed of course!" cried Prince Purpletights. "You can tell she's a real princess if a pea in the bed keeps her awake."

"I do not pee in my bed!" cried the princess indignantly.

But the princes were not listening. "Kissy kissy!" they slurped, reaching out for her.

"Unhand my darling Rapunzel, you swine!" cried Prince Greentights as he scrambled over the balcony.

"Where did you come from?" gasped the princess.

"Fellow called Honest Jack swapped me three magic beans for the Crown Jewels," replied the prince. "I just climbed up the beanstalk and here I am."

And indeed a gigantic beanstalk had suddenly appeared outside, towering over the apartment block and vanishing into the clouds.

"Well," said Prince Purpletights doubtfully, "there are three of us and only one of her so I suppose we'll just have to fight to the death."

"Oh . . . er . . . well . . . no, that's hardly necessary is it?" stammered Prince Yellowtights. "I mean, one of us might get hurt!"

"We could raffle her, I suppose," suggested Prince Greentights.

"I know," said Prince Purpletights, "Think of a number between one and ten and —"

"Now look here!" said the princess. "If you think —"

"What's that smell?" said Prince Greentights suddenly.

"What's that growling sound?" said Prince Yellowtights.

"What's that huge hairy thing coming in the door?" said Prince Purpletights.

"THE BEAST!" screamed all three princes and bolted for the balcony.

"GROOAR!" roared the Beast, charging after them. "You leave my Beauty alone!"

In a trice the three terrified princes were scrambling down the beanstalk with the bellowing Beast in hot pursuit.

But as the princess rushed to the edge of the balcony to watch the chase, a voice even mightier than the Beast's thundered from somewhere in the clouds:

"FEE FI FO FUM, I'M COMING DOWN TO BITE YOUR BUM!"

"The Giant!" shrieked the three princes, and even the Beast looked worried.

"Don't worry," cried the princess, "there's a boy down there with an axe chopping down the beanstalk!"

"Jack!" screamed the three princes. "Don't do it, Jack!"

The Beast whimpered.

The Giant thundered.

The axe chopped.

The beanstalk swayed, creaked, cracked and fell.

Screams, howls, thuds, silence.

"Oh, dear!" said the princess, as she peered over the balcony.

Far, far below a giant was sitting in the middle of the street rubbing his head and looking puzzled.

Presently three very squashed looking princes crawled from beneath his great fat bottom, carrying a groaning beast between them.

"Come on lads," said Prince Purpletights. "Let's go back to the forest."

"But there are dragons there!" said Prince Greentights.

"And ogres," said Prince Yellowtights.

"And spiders," muttered the Beast, who didn't like creepy-crawlies.

"True," said Prince Purpletights. "But at least there aren't any princesses."

So the three princes, the Beast and the Giant returned to the forest and the princess stayed in her tower block. From time to time, her fairy godmother appeared to invite her to a ball, but the princess would not go. Occasionally, her wicked stepmother turned up with poisoned apples, but the princess never ate them. And once, she woke to find a frog sitting on her pillow blinking at her.

"If you kiss me," said the frog, "I'll turn into a handsome prince."

"If you don't go away," replied the princess, "I'll flush you down the loo!"

That was the last time she ever found a frog in her bed, and though she did marry somebody one day, he wasn't handsome, he wasn't a prince and he never, ever wore tights!

FINBAR O'CONNOR

Finbar O'Connor lives in Dublin, where he is currently studying for a law degree. His wife Margaret is a barrister, and he too hopes to practise law when he graduates next year. He has written for children's TV, for primary school textbooks and anthologies of poetry and songs, and has contributed a prizewinning children's story to a collection published in Ireland. He also sings and plays guitar and keyboards in a rock band.

He says: "My earliest childhood memory is of my father telling me fairy tales at bedtime – some traditional and some of his own devising. I have always incorporated the characters and characteristics of these tales in my own stories – adding humour because I regard it as an essential ingredient in children's fiction."

The Howling Hills

Alan Stone

Illustrated by
Ian Beck

To all my children

Many years ago, long before you or I were born, a community of forest people lived contentedly in a warm valley, hidden from the rest of the world at the bottom of a deep ravine. Each day the men speared fish in the river and hunted the wild beasts. The women collected berries and roots, and the children played happily in the sunlit glades.

Many kinds of wild creature roamed the forested hills which surrounded the valley, but none of them ever bothered the people. That is, until the day – or rather the night – a strange new creature had arrived. Its fearful howls resounded across the valley each night as it roamed the dark hills. Curiously, nobody had actually seen the creature. This was because old Ipok, the village headman, had warned them about its fierceness and had forbidden them ever to wander into the hills after dark. But every night the villagers would tremble in their beds as they listened to the brute's cries.

For many years the villagers lived in fear of the creature they had never seen. Those who had been children when the howling had begun were now young men and women.

One day, the great gong echoed through the valley, calling the people to gather in the open place in front of Ipok's hut. Eventually the old man appeared and raised his arms above his head to silence their chatter. He leaned on his staff and gripped it tightly with both hands as the young maiden by his side helped him to sit on a low stool.

At last Ipok spoke. "Good people, all of you know my daughter." He smiled fondly at the girl. People nodded. Many had known Esmeralda since she had been a small child. She was admired by everyone, for she was gentle and kind and beautiful. Her long hair was as black as a raven's feathers and her green eyes glittered like emeralds. They also knew, alas, that she was born mute and could only speak by means of smiles and frowns and other signs.

Ipok continued. "Esmeralda has reached her nineteenth year and it is time for her to marry.

That is why the great gong has called you here today. I wish to find out which of our young men is the bravest, for it is he who shall be my daughter's husband."

The moment he had finished speaking, a tall figure stepped forward. Ipok surveyed him for a moment. "Who are you?" he demanded. The man replied, "My name is Rib. Let no one in this valley dare claim that he is braver than I!" He stamped both feet in the dust and leapt high in the air, growling like a panther. Then he posed stiffly like a stone statue, his eyes fixed on Ipok. Esmeralda simply smiled.

A second man, with a tangle of black hair and a curly moustache, spoke out with equal boldness. "I am Rut, brother of Rib, and my courage is boundless!" He jumped into the air and landed on his back, rolling over and over in the red dust, grunting like a wild pig. Then he too stood stiff and silent. Ipok's daughter smiled again.

There was a pause. The old man was about to speak when a third man stepped forward. He was still only a youth, no older than Esmeralda herself. He said simply, "My name is Ratak-Tak. I have loved Esmeralda for as long as I can remember and I will marry her if she will have me."

Ipok studied the three men, his glance darting from one to the other. He frowned. "Clearly, you cannot all marry my daughter, so I will have to set you a test." The three listened intently. The old man continued. "Whichever one of you first brings me proof that he has performed a feat of the utmost bravery, then that man shall become Esmeralda's husband."

When the two brothers heard this they grinned at Ratak-Tak. Rib scoffed, "You will never win her, o young one!" Rut turned to his brother. "And neither will you!" he cried, and without another word he ran off into the forest. The others knew that they must wait.

Before the day was much older, Rut returned, carrying across his shoulder a panther, its breast pierced by a spear. He threw the dead beast at Ipok's feet. "See!" he cried. "I have killed a fierce panther. Now I will marry your daughter." The old man turned to Esmeralda, but she only smiled at him and shook her head. Then Ipok said to Rut, "My daughter says that it takes little courage to kill a panther when you are armed with a long spear."

When Rib saw that his brother had failed he called out, "Now we shall see who is the bravest!" and went off in the direction of the river. He too soon returned, dragging behind him a crocodile so huge that only with difficulty could he pull it through the village, leaving behind a trail of yellow mud. Rib stood before the old man grinning, his teeth gleaming white below his moustache. "I have no need of weapons," he boasted. "I wrestled in the swamp with this ferocious beast and killed it with my bare hands." But again Esmeralda smiled at her father and shook her head. Ipok turned to Rib. "I am sorry, but my daughter says that anyone can wrestle with a crocodile in the heat of the day when it would rather sleep than fight!"

By now the sun was sinking behind the hills which surrounded the valley. Ratak-Tak spoke. "Ipok, I understand well that I must carry out a deed of extreme daring if I am to win your daughter. If you will wait until tomorrow morning you will find out just how brave I am, despite my youth." The old man nodded his agreement and the young one bade him farewell.

Ratak-Tak looked up at the shadowy hills which rose like purple clouds above him. He recalled

Ipok's warning of long ago that no one should go up into the hills after dark lest they come face to face with the strange creature which prowled there. Only last night he had been awakened by its shrill howling. But the memory of Esmeralda's smile gave him the courage he needed. He started up the slope.

It was dark beneath the trees and Ratak-Tak was barely able to see the path which rose upwards through the gloom. The way became steeper. The night grew darker. His nostrils were filled with the familiar leafy smells of the damp forest. He climbed on. He stopped to watch as the moon emerged for a moment from behind a cloud, like a silver saucer floating in the sky, then disappeared again. The night seemed even darker than before. Ratak-Tak stood still and listened. He thought he could hear a distant moaning. Yes! A long, low wailing sound. He shivered. Then all was silent again.

Suddenly there was a piercing scream. And another. And another. The howling had begun.

Ratak-Tak trembled, but he continued through the forest, climbing towards the place from which the noises seemed to come. Still higher he climbed, until the howling rang so loud in his ears that he knew

some fearsome creature must be near. All at once the howling stopped. In the sudden silence he could hear the pounding of his heart. He stayed quite still, crouching on the ground, sensing that something, some breathing creature, was close to him, waiting, watching in the blackness which enclosed them both. Then a sudden yell made him jump and he saw a shape plunge through the shadows directly ahead of him. He caught a brief glimpse of the creature's wild eyes and its long, tangled mane. "I am doomed unless I act quickly," he said to himself.

Tensing his muscles, he sprang up and pounced upon the shape in front of him. The creature hissed and howled. He felt its claws snatch at his face. Again and again the writhing creature clawed and scratched, making him cry out in pain, but it could not escape his grip. With his right hand he felt for his hunting knife and with a great effort managed to draw it from his belt. He struck hard. The thing in his arms uttered a strange moan, gasped, and fell heavy and limp to the forest floor. The night was silent once again.

Ratak-Tak, sweating and breathing heavily, bent over the dead shape lying in the dark shadows at his feet. Without stopping to rest he heaved it across his back and began the difficult journey down the hillside, feeling his way slowly in the darkness. The creature's damp mane hung limply against his skin.

It was still dark when he finally got to the village. He staggered through the low entrance of his dwelling and flung his heavy burden to the ground. He was exhausted, but hardly pausing to catch his breath he made his way to Ipok's hut and called out, "It is I, Ratak-Tak. I have slain the howling monster of the hills which has terrified our people for so many years. Now I demand Esmeralda as my wife!" The words echoed between the rows of huts. He waited for an answer.

The new day's sun was edging the rim of the valley with pale gold. Ratak-Tak was glad to feel its warmth on his face. He listened to the clatters and creaks as the villagers unbolted their doors. The door of Ipok's hut slowly opened and the old man appeared. Ratak-Tak looked at him and said, "Go and fetch your daughter. My courageous deed must be rewarded as you promised."

By now several villagers had gathered in front of Ipok's hut. They had heard the young man's boast and were eager to find out whether he spoke the truth. A mocking voice called out, "Show us the loathsome creature's body or we shall not believe you!" It was Rib. "Yes. Show us the proof!" cried Rut, his brother. More villagers had gathered. "SHOW US!" they all cried. Ratak-Tak looked upon the crowd. "Follow me!" he commanded. He led them through the village and when they reached his dwelling he ordered them to wait. "Inside is the body of the fearsome creature which I captured and killed. I will bring it out to you so you may see for yourselves the claws that made my wounds, the shaggy mane, the shining eyes." He stooped through the low doorway of his hut. The villagers waited in silence. They waited for several minutes then began to grow impatient. "THE BEAST! BRING OUT THE BEAST!" went up the cry.

What happened next took them by surprise. They saw Ratak-Tak stagger from his hut, his hands clasped to his face. Tears were rolling down his cheeks. "What is this?" mocked Rib and Rut. "The bravest man in the valley, weeping?" The poor young man dropped to his knees and wept pitifully. The brothers looked at each other in amazement then strode across to the entrance of the hut to peer inside. Through the gloom they could just make out a dark shape sprawled on the floor, a hunting knife jutting from its middle. As their eyes became accustomed to the dim light they began to see more clearly. What they saw was indeed a body, but it was not the carcass of some cursed monster with a tangled black mane, not the corpse of some terrifying creature of the night. They gasped in utter horror at what they now saw. They saw the body of a girl, the beautiful face draped in the long black tresses of her hair. Her eyes were the colour of emeralds. It was Esmeralda.

At that moment, old Ipok himself stooped through the doorway of the hut. For a long time he looked in silence at the sprawling shape, then with a heavy sigh he turned and shuffled outside. He lowered himself to the ground where Ratak-Tak was kneeling. Neither of them spoke.

The dreadful news soon spread among the crowd. Old men, young men, women and children, they all wept openly. They formed a circle round Ipok and Ratak-Tak, waiting for some kind of explanation.

The old headman, looking more ancient than ever, said nothing for a long while. Finally, he rose shakily to his feet. Leaning heavily on his staff he lifted his eyes to the sky and spoke softly, "Sleep, my daughter, and may your rest be sweet." Then turning his gaze on those gathered around him, he said, "Poor Esmeralda, my wordless child, who grew up to be the gentle lady you all knew. Her heart was filled with the sweet words she could not speak and her spirit with the songs she could not sing. So every night she left my house and by darkness wandered in the hills, and there in the thick forest tried to set free a few imprisoned sounds. But her voice would not obey her heart and her only songs were the anguished howls that echoed through the valley and wrought fear in those who heard. For many years I guarded her sad secret. And then, when at last she came of age, I hoped that some man brave enough to face this truth would take her for his wife. But Esmeralda now is dead. No longer will your sleep be broken by the howling from the hills."

Esmeralda was laid to rest at the foot of the hill from which Ratak-Tak had borne her. A garden of white roses was planted there to mark the place.

Ratak-Tak often visited that sad and beautiful garden. He would stand in silence while the sun lowered its glow behind the valley rim, as it had always done. Sometimes he would imagine that he could hear the distant sound of Esmeralda's wild singing echoing from hill to hill in the darkness, but it would only be the soft song of the birds as they settled in their nests, or the whistling of the wind through the leaves.

Alan Stone

Alan Stone lives in North London with his wife and three children. He works for the Medical Research Council and has been writing scientific and technical publications since 1961, but this is his first piece of published writing for children.

He says: "When my first child, Richard, was two years old I used to tell him a different bedtime story every night. Once we had done The Three Bears, Little Red Riding Hood and the like, it was generally easier for me to make up original stories spontaneously than to try to remember traditional ones. This ritual did however become more challenging as he got older, so the stories tended to become progressively more complex. A brand new story every night. That was the expectation I had to fulfil with Richard, then with Julia, and no doubt this will continue with Robert when he is a little older. There have been literally hundreds of little tales, and it is fortunate that my wife persuaded me to write down a few of them. The Howling Hills is one of these survivors."

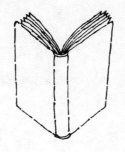

We All Belong to Glasgow

Ann Burnett

Illustrated by
Sami Sweeten

To Ronan and Christopher

One day when Jimmy Patel came home from school, he saw his mum and the neighbours talking together at the mouth of the close where he lived in the south side of Glasgow.

"It's diabolical," his mum was saying. "You can't have that here."

"Can't we complain?" said Teresa di Paolo. "Have we not got any say in it at all?"

"It shouldn't be allowed." Mr Levy was shaking his head.

"I'd rather the flat was left empty than have them here," said Seamus Kane.

"What's wrong?" Jimmy asked.

"Well," said his mum, "the Council are putting a family into the empty flat on the bottom and" – here she paused and bent her head closer to his ear – "they're a family of ALIENS!"

The word hissed out of her mouth.

"What's an alien?" Jimmy asked.

"They're from up there." Teresa raised her eyes skywards. "Outer space."

"Are there any wee boys to play with?" Jimmy said.

"You'll not be playing with the likes of them even if there are hundreds of wee boys," said his mum. "No son of mine is going to be playing with one of them."

Just then, Heather McLeod came into the close wheeling her baby Gemma in her pram.

"It's all right for you," she said. "But I'm going to have them living right across from me."

Jimmy left them tutting and sighing and went into his room to think about the new family. He wondered what they would look like. He'd never met an alien although he'd seen them on television.

A few days later the family moved in. There were two larger aliens and a wee one about the same size as Jimmy. He couldn't wait to see if it was someone he could play with. He ran down the stairs and nearly bumped into the biggest alien who was carrying a strange bundle of tubing and helmets into the flat.

"Sorry," gasped Jimmy, bending down to pick up a purple tube the alien had dropped. Then he saw the wee alien peering out of the door at him.

"Hullo," Jimmy said. "Are you coming out to play? Fancy a game of keepie-uppy?"

The wee alien changed from green to bright pink and said something in a whisper.

"How do you change colour?" asked Jimmy. "Can you teach me to do that?"

"He is shy," said the big alien in a funny, quiet voice. "It is all strange here."

At that moment, Heather McLeod came up the steps into the close.

"You come away from there, Jimmy Patel," she yelled. "Your mammy told you not to speak to them."

Jimmy hesitated. The big alien shooed the wee alien into the flat and closed the door.

"You keep away from them Jimmy," said Heather. "They shouldn't be mixing with the likes of us."

Jimmy sadly kicked his football around the back green. The wee alien had looked as if he might come out to play and Jimmy would have liked to learn how to change colour like he did.

Suddenly the wee alien was standing beside him.

"How did you do that?" Jimmy asked.

"I come through wall," said the wee alien.

"I wish I could do that," said Jimmy. "That would

be great. What's your name?"

"Gooroly Schluff," said the wee alien in his funny, quiet voice. "What's yours?"

"Jimmy Patel," said Jimmy. "Fancy a game of keepie-uppy?"

"You teach me," said Gooroly.

"You just keep the ball in the air with your feet or head," said Jimmy. "See how long we can do it for."

Gooroly turned out to be very good at keepie-uppy as he used air jets all over his body to puff the ball up in the air. Jimmy was impressed.

"I wish I could do that," said Jimmy. "You're awfy good at it."

Gooroly turned orange with pleasure.

"And I wish I could do that too," he said.

Just then, his mum threw open the kitchen window and yelled down, "Jimmy, come up for your dinner!"

Gooroly silently disappeared through the wall into his own flat.

"See you later," Jimmy whispered as he picked up the ball and ran into the close.

"Who were you talking to out there?" asked his mum as she dished up his dinner.

"Gooroly," mumbled Jimmy through a mouthful of beans and potatoes. "Do you know what he can do? He can —"

"Have you been playing with that alien? What did I tell you? You're not to play with him, do you hear me?"

"But why, Mum?" wailed Jimmy. "He's good fun and he's nice and —"

"They're not like us," said his mum. "You don't know what kind of germs you can pick up from them."

But Jimmy played with Gooroly whenever he could. He would stand outside Gooroly's bedroom and whisper his name and Gooroly would come through the wall. Then they would sneak out to the back lane and play there until it was time to go in or they heard someone coming. Jimmy knew that if any of the neighbours saw him with Gooroly they would tell his mum.

Once when Heather was hanging out the washing in the back green, the door to her flat slammed shut in the wind.

"I'm locked out," she said anxiously to Jimmy, "and Gemma's in there on her own."

"I'll get Gooroly," he said.

In less than a minute Gooroly had slipped through the wall and into Heather's flat. When he opened the door, he was holding a smiling Gemma and blowing gentle little puffs of air at her from his air jets.

Heather snatched her out of Gooroly's arms and

rushed into her flat without even thanking him.

"That was awfy rude," said Jimmy. "My mum is always telling me —"

Gooroly put his hand on Jimmy's arm. "It does not matter," he said softly.

Jimmy was sad that he couldn't play openly with Gooroly and have him up to his flat to play with his computer. He had once been into Gooroly's flat and he'd been fascinated by the tubes and helmets all around.

"We find it hard to breathe easily here," said Gooroly's dad. "It is nice to breathe the air of our home sometimes."

Jimmy was also embarrassed by the adults' unfriendliness. They wouldn't even say hullo to Gooroly's family and were constantly complaining about them.

"The smells that come from their cooking are disgusting," said Heather McLeod.

"They make all sorts of strange noises," said Seamus Kane. "Really weird sounds."

"I wish they'd use the door like everybody else instead of melting through walls," complained Mr Levy. "It's not natural."

"We should do something about them," said Teresa. "They should be sent back to their planet or

at least go and live somewhere else."

"Let's have a meeting," said Jimmy's mum. "In our flat. Tonight."

By half-past seven everybody was squeezed into the Patels' front room. Heather had brought up some scones she had made and Teresa came with a jar of her home-made raspberry jam.

"Thank you," said Jimmy's mum. "Just what we need with a cup of tea."

But Jimmy was unhappy. He didn't want any harm or hurt to come to Gooroly and his family.

"You make a good cup of tea," Teresa said as Jimmy's mum handed her a cup. "I always drank coffee at home but I like tea now."

"Where is home?" Jimmy asked.

"Italy," said Teresa. "Although I was born here, I still think of Italy as home."

"My grandpa and granny came from Pakistan," said Jimmy.

"Indeed they did," said Jimmy's mum, "and what a time of it they had. They didn't speak a word of English."

"Neither did I," said Mr Levy. "I came from Germany when I was three. My parents spoke Yiddish at home but my new friends spoke English."

"When my father came over from Ireland, nobody could understand his accent," said Seamus Kane. "And he was very lonely for a long while until he made some friends."

"So none of us belongs to Glasgow," said Jimmy's mum, "except you, Heather."

"Well, no," said Heather. "Actually I'm from Edinburgh."

"Really?" said Jimmy's mum, still holding the teapot. "Edinburgh? Will you be wanting more tea then?"

"Isn't that funny?" said Seamus Kane. "All of our families came to Glasgow to live."

"Just like Gooroly and his family," shouted Jimmy. "They're no different from any of us."

There was a silence broken only by the humming of the fridge in the kitchen. Everybody stared at Jimmy. He felt his face turning bright red. Nobody spoke for what seemed like ages. Seamus Kane lowered his eyes and picked at his fingernail while Teresa chewed her lip. Mr Levy wiped his nose on a handkerchief and Jimmy's mum brushed at a crumb on her lap. Jimmy's face was burning but he gripped his chair tightly and stood his ground.

"Och, Jimmy," said Heather softly. "You've changed colour. Just like Gooroly."

Everyone laughed and then Mr Levy said, "The boy is quite right. The Schluffs are strangers as we all were once and we should be kind to them as people were to us when we came to Scotland."

"We didn't think, did we?" said Teresa. "The Schluffs must have thought we weren't very nice."

"I was very rude to Gooroly when I was locked out of my flat," said Heather. "I'm sorry now."

Jimmy's mum said, "Jimmy, just you away down to the Schluffs and ask them if they'd like to join us for a cup of tea. There's plenty left in the pot."

Jimmy raced down the stairs and rang the Schluffs' bell. "Would you all like to come up for a cup of tea?" he said.

The Schluffs changed from green to orange with pleasure and followed Jimmy up the stairs to his flat.

"Come away in," said Jimmy's mum as the Schluffs shyly peered round the door. "Have a cup of tea with us."

"And try one of my scones," said Heather. "I baked them this morning."

"Yes," said Mrs Schluff. "I smell them."

"I bet it smelled funny to you," said Mr Levy. "I remember when I too thought that the cooking smells were strange here."

Jimmy and Gooroly left the grown-ups to it and headed into Jimmy's bedroom to play on his computer.

Heather brought in a plate of scones spread with Teresa's raspberry jam.

"I forgot to thank you for helping me that day," she said to Gooroly. "Perhaps you'd like to come in and play with Gemma again. She liked when you blew puffs of air at her."

Gooroly turned bright pink and then orange.

"Did you know I changed colour today?" said Jimmy. "I went bright red."

"That was awfy good," said Gooroly. "Pure dead brilliant."

Jimmy stared at him. "You're beginning to talk like me."

"I belong to Glasgow too," said Gooroly.

"We *all* belong to Glasgow," said Jimmy.

ANN BURNETT

Ann Burnett was born in Glasgow. After teaching in Canada and Australia, she returned to Scotland and now lives and teaches in Ayrshire. She started writing when she stopped work to have her family and has now written children's annuals and contributed to anthologies, as well as writing for BBC radio schools' broadcasts. She enjoys gardening, reading and swimming and has two sons, aged fifteen and eleven.

She says: "I joined the Ayr Writers' Club and started writing for children because I thought it only required a few hundred words compared with 60,000 for a novel. Little did I realize I'd picked the harder option. I enjoy writing for young children because I have to explain (sometimes) quite hard concepts in a way they will understand. And sometimes I manage it and sometimes I fail miserably. But I keep on trying. I also like being able to combine reality and fantasy, and different ideas and situations in new and interesting ways."

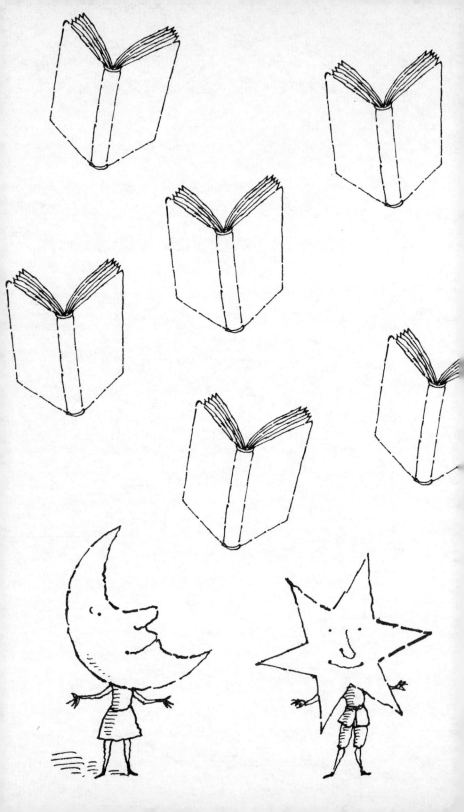

Do you want to read more of the best children's stories?

If you enjoyed *Story of the Year 2*, then you'll want to read the first ever *Story of the Year*. It contains 1993's winning entries for six to nine-year-olds. There's the prizewinning *Kevin the Blue* and nine other exciting stories – from highflying go-carts to down-to-earth goose girls – once again with artwork by top children's illustrators.

Funny and touching, exciting and magical, these are the Stories of the Year, 1993.

There will be another Story of the Year competition in Spring 1995, so watch the *Independent* for details . . .